D0566314

1012

HIGH FRONTIER
SCHOOL LIBRARY

STEPHANIE S. TOLAN

FLIGHT OF THE RAVEN

HARPERCOLLINS*PUBLISHERS*

Flight of the Raven
Copyright © 2001 by Stephanie S. Tolan
All rights reserved. No part of this book may be used or reproduced in any manner whatsoever without written permission except in the case of brief quotations embodied in critical articles and reviews.
Printed in the United States of America. For information address HarperCollins Children's Books, a division of HarperCollins Publishers, 1350 Avenue of the Americas, New York, NY 10019.
www.harperchildrens.com

Library of Congress Cataloging-in-Publication Data
Tolan, Stephanie S.
Flight of the raven / by Stephanie S. Tolan.
p. cm.
Summary: Elijah, a nine-year-old African American with unusual mental powers and a special ability to reach into the natural world, becomes a hostage of a terrorist militia group and finds himself in a world of violence.
ISBN 0-688-17419-1 — ISBN 0-06-029620-8 (lib. bdg.)
[1. Militia movements—Fiction. 2. Terrorism—Fiction. 3. Government, Resistance to—Fiction. 4. Extrasensory perception—Fiction. 5. Human-animal communication—Fiction. 6. African Americans—Fiction.] I. Title.
PZ7.T5735 Fl 2001
[Fic]—dc21 00-054043
CIP
AC

Typography by Alison Donalty
Spot art by Sasha Illingworth
1 2 3 4 5 6 7 8 9 10
❖
First Edition

To all the real Ark Kids who are among us—

those who have recognized themselves and those who haven't yet.

You'll discover your quest when the time is right!

Grateful acknowledgment to the many people who helped the raven to fly:

Elisabet Sahtouris, evolution biologist and friend, who has helped me stretch my view of reality, and Puma Quispe Singona, Peruvian medicine man in training, who so warmly opens windows into his powerful world;

Robert W. Tolan, Jr., M.D., our family infectious disease specialist, who connected me with all the information I needed to imagine biowar;

Barry and Trudy, who once again provided time in the Adirondacks to fill my mind and heart with sounds and smells and images, and who let me borrow from their prodigious book collection what I needed for research;

Jack Monigan, who not only found the *real* Paradise Park and took me for a tour but also brought his police and antiterrorist task-force experience to the tough questions, and asked others I hadn't yet considered.

And to those whose writing was essential:

Bernd Heinrich, whose study of ravens has given us so much of what we know about these extraordinary birds;

John Perkins, whose book *Shapeshifting* provided a critical bridge from one perspective to another.

HIGH FRONTIER
SCHOOL LIBRARY

part one

militia

DAY ONE

Amber Landis pushed her blond hair behind her ears and wiped the sweat from her forehead. It was hot and muggy in the basement computer room. It was also dark. The only light was a crack of sunlight at one side of the narrow window up near the ceiling where the blind had curled at its edge. She hadn't turned on the light because she wasn't really supposed to be there.

"Wait," her father had said when he left the compound. "Look after your brother, do what Cassie says, and just wait. When news of the mission gets onto the nets, it'll be full of lies. I'll tell you all about it when I get back."

"But what *is* the mission?" she had asked. He hadn't answered. He'd only gone to join the group of camouflage-clad men milling around the truck that was revving its engine in front of the old barn.

There are things you're better off not knowing, she'd heard all her life. She hated it. Hated it, hated it, hated it! How would she ever be part of her father's mission, how would she ever make a difference in the world, if she wasn't even allowed to know what they were doing till after it was done?

Cassie, her stepmother, knew, and she was worried. She was doing her best not to show it, giving Amber and Kenny their stupid homeschool assignments as if everything was perfectly normal. But she had taken the radio into her room as soon as the men left, and Amber knew she listened to it early every morning and late every night. Amber couldn't understand why nobody wanted her and Kenny to know what was going on even now, when it surely had to be over, or nearly over. It wasn't as if they'd tell anybody. It wasn't as if there was anybody to tell. Since the men had left, she had not seen one single person except Kenny and Cassie.

She'd thought about the possibility that this mission was so much more dangerous than usual that something bad—really bad—might happen. If that was true, Cassie might be trying to protect them from finding out. Amber couldn't see what difference it would make when or how they found out about it if the news was that bad.

The mission was different from anything the Free Mountain Militia had ever done before. Different and very, very big. That she knew. For weeks the air had been charged with a new energy as the men had prepared for it. There had never been so much coming and going from the compound, lots of it at night.

It was the fifth day since the men had driven away in the truck, her father following in his black Honda. Five long, hot days. No mission had ever taken that long. Amber was tired of wondering, tired of waiting, and even more tired of trying to look after Kenny. Her ten-year-old brother insisted he was a soldier, a soldier who didn't need looking after. Especially not by a sister only two years older than he was. "You're just a *girl*," he'd sneered that very morning when she reminded him he wasn't allowed to go out in the canoe without a life jacket. "You can't tell me what to do." So he'd gone without the life jacket. If he drowned, it wouldn't be her fault.

She listened at the door for a moment, then clicked the lock on the doorknob and switched on the computer. When it had run through its wake-up pattern, she sat down and took herself out onto the nets. And found immediately the lies her father had warned her about:

>Path:

>Laurel.grt.com!news.amherst.edu!news.mtholyoke.

>edu!111-winkenllnl.gov!agate!bass!clarinews

>From: clarinews@clarinet.com (AP)

>Message-ID: <militiaUR237_eb6@clarinet.com>

>Date: Thurs, 10 Aug 00 8:34:50EDT

>

>PLATTSBURGH, NY (AP) No leads have been

>reported in the most devastating terrorist attack ever
>launched against American citizens in their own
>country, bigger even than the bombing of the federal
>building in Oklahoma City. The death toll from the
>bombing of two overpasses on Interstate 87, the
>highway known locally as the Northway, has risen to
>183 with the confirmation that two buses carrying
>Canadian tourists home from a visit to DisneyWorld
>were among the vehicles lost in the bomb blasts and
>the ensuing explosion of a gasoline tanker truck.
>According to sources, identification of bodies will not
>be completed for some time, but both buses were
>carrying 45 passengers.
>   The Free Mountain Militia, an anarchist fringe
>group never before suspected of terrorism, has taken
>credit for the bombing. Local police have been joined
>by the FBI, the National Guard, and large numbers
>of citizen volunteers in an all-out search of the area
>surrounding the highway south to Lake George and
>north to the Canadian border, where the RCMP is
>conducting its own search.
>   United States President Daniel Harris and
>Canadian Premier Jacques Martier both arrived this
>morning to survey the scene of the devastation and
>are assuring their citizens that the perpetrators of

>this atrocity will be found and dealt with to the
>fullest extent of the law.
> In an unrelated story, an eight-year-old African-
>American boy suffering from autism has disappeared
>from Laurel Mountain, a private mental institution
>near the site of the bomb blast, and is lost in the
>extensive Adirondack wilderness where the search
>for the terrorists is being conducted. A separate
>search has not been initiated for the boy; searchers
>have been asked to keep an eye out for him as they
>go. "We're determined to cover every square inch of
>forest," National Guard Officer Lester Cunningham
>has said. "There's no way we'll miss that little boy in
>the process."

Amber read the piece again. Lies, her father had said. Of course. The government always lied, and the media were controlled by the government. She knew that. She'd always known it. But which were the lies?

The line of five men in camouflage fatigues was moving quickly through the forest, guided upward on the mountain not by a trail but by compass reckoning. In spite of the dense shade under the trees, the heat was oppressive, and they were soaked with sweat. No one spoke as they moved, one or another taking a quick drink from a canteen now and again. It was well past noon, and they'd been on the move since dawn, stopping only for small rest breaks and to listen briefly to a battery-operated radio.

Suddenly the man in the lead, dark hair curling out from beneath his camouflage cap, stopped, and the man behind him nearly ran up his back. Behind them the others came to a ragged stop, looking at one another questioningly. "What's up?" the second man whispered.

The other didn't answer. He merely pointed. A huge moss-covered tree was lying at an angle, its upper branches caught among other trees, a tangle of roots nearly head high reaching into the air from a mound of moss and ferns. Next to the roots, spaced next to each other as neatly as if they'd been placed beside a bed before retiring, stood a small pair of ragged navy blue sneakers. The dark-haired man, a finger to his lips, motioned to the others to fan out around the tree. They did so, indicating with no more than raised eyebrows and shrugs their question about what they were doing.

The leader bent to peer under the trunk, where a mass of fir branches stuck out, their tips at odd angles almost as if they'd been woven together. He took hold of one branch, moved it slightly so that the others moved as well, and then waited. After a moment he gave a gentle tug, again moving the tangle of branches and pulling the one he was holding a few inches toward him so that a small opening appeared behind it. He looked through the opening and then stood up, nodding.

"What?" the man next to him mouthed.

"What are the odds?" the dark-haired man said, his voice at normal volume now. "A few yards either way, and we'd have missed him."

"Missed who?"

"That black kid who ran away from the mental hospital. The one they've been talking about on the news. Not that it does him or us any good. He's dead. Must've fixed himself a bed here last night. Can't imagine what killed him; it wasn't cold." The man began pulling branches out from under the tree trunk and gestured for help. After a few moments they could all see what he had seen. A small barefoot boy, a metal bracelet around one ankle, wearing blue jeans and a red-and-white-striped T-shirt, lay curled in a fetal position, one dark fist clutched tightly beneath his chin, the other over his head as if to protect himself from a possible blow.

"Leave him," a blond man with a flat, smooth face said, kicking at the pile of branches they had pulled free. "Dump those shoes in there with him, and put the branches back. We don't need nobody else finding him and seeing that somebody besides the kid was here. This whole place'll be crawling with feds and soldiers soon enough."

The dark-haired man stood for a moment, looking down at the tiny figure, frowning. "Too bad," he said. "We could've taken him along. Kept him as a hostage. A trade. You never know what sort of bargaining chip you might need." He took his cap off and ran a hand through the hair that was stuck to his neck with sweat. "I have an idea. Get a picture of him, Ham. Nobody would know he isn't just sleeping. He looks peaceful enough."

The man he'd spoken to, heavyset and crew-cut, nodded and pulled open a side pocket on his pack to take out a 35-mm camera. He stepped closer and bent to get a good shot in the shadows. When the flash went off, the boy stirred. The movement wasn't large, and the child didn't open his eyes. But he'd moved. They'd all seen it.

The leader leaned in and laid a finger against the boy's throat. "He's got a pulse. Very slow, but steady."

"So?" the flat-faced man said. "We can't drag some little kid back with us; we got too far to go."

"Of course we can, Virgil," the dark-haired man said. He put his cap back on and reached down to pull the boy from his nest. The child made no sound, but his body uncurled as he was dragged free of his hiding place. The arm he'd had over his head moved to join the other, its fist still clutched tightly under his chin. "Wake up, kid!" the man said, and tried to stand the boy on his legs. He might as well have tried to stand a rag doll. "Well, give me a hand with him, somebody!"

The man named Ham reached to help, taking the boy under the arms and slinging him against his shoulder as the other man stood, brushing the leaves and dirt from his knees.

"I'm tellin' you, Mack, we should leave him," the blond man said. "There's something wrong with him. He was in a loony bin, after all. You don't know what kind of trouble he could be. Besides, he's a *black* kid!"

The leader turned on him. "You better not let Landis hear you sounding like a racist. He'd have you outa the Cadre, out of the Militia for that matter, before you could blink."

The blond man kicked at a rock, his face flushing pink. "Ah, who said anything racist, for cripe sake? I just said he was black. He *is* black!"

"Yeah, well, the operative word here is *kid*. People want lost kids back. As long as he's alive and tradable, he could come in handy. We're taking him." He looked from one to the other of the rest of the men. "Anybody else have any objections?"

The others shook their heads.

"Okay, then. Let's get going. Somebody get his shoes."

When they'd rearranged their packs, they went on, moving as steadily and swiftly as before. There was no sound from the child and no movement. He had not opened his eyes. As he was carried roughly, slung over Ham's shoulder, he kept one hand, fist tightly closed, tucked under his chin.

From the top of a white pine next to the fallen tree, a raven lifted itself silently into the air and flew over the men as they moved.

When Elijah felt himself pulled from his nest beneath the tree, rough hands dragging him into a world of sunlight and the roar that was and was not sound, the roar of violence he had been running from when he left Laurel Mountain filled his head again, louder than he'd ever heard it. He kept his eyes tightly shut, let himself go limp. *Mountain*, he thought, trying to retreat into the consciousness of the great stone presence. Men's voices intruded, but he blocked them out. *Mountain! Silence!*

He felt himself lifted and flung across the hard shoulder of a man whose huge hand clasped his legs as they began moving. Elijah's head jolted with every step the man took. Tree branches brushed at his back. Clutching his marble tightly, Elijah reached with his mind, sending it out into the mountain until he could hear nothing, feel nothing. Concentrating with fierce intensity, Elijah Raymond turned himself to stone.

Amber heard the truck engine laboring up the long hill and the wheels scattering gravel. "It's them!" she yelled. "They're back!" She leaped off the porch steps and ran to stand in front of the barn, where she could see the truck the moment it made the last turn out from under the trees. She put a hand up to shade her eyes against the sun, still hot and still bright, which was resting on the edge of Bald Hill. It sounded like only the truck coming, no car behind, but her father would be in it, surely. He had to be.

The screen door behind her banged, and Kenny came out onto the porch, followed by Cassie, wiping her hands on a dish towel, her dark face impassive, her eyes fixed intently on the gravel road. Kenny, a chocolate chip cookie in one hand, was stuffing another into his mouth. Amber hadn't been able to eat the beans and tomatoes and hamburgers they'd had for dinner, and the cookies hadn't tempted her. Her mind had been too full of the story she had read on the nets, the story she wasn't supposed to know about. Cassie had asked her to string the beans for dinner, and she'd watched Cassie shape the hamburgers, slapping the meat with a kind of tense ferocity. Her stepmother had been even more silent than usual, distant and preoccupied as if her mind too was on a story that was part truth, part media lies.

At the table, while Kenny groused about not having caught any fish, Amber had sat, pushing her food around her plate and worrying. Everyone knew Charles Landis headed the Free Mountain Militia. Were the cops and the feds looking for him now? Had they found him already? And if not, would they come here? And if they did come, what would happen then?

The truck appeared at last, its gray and green and brown camouflage tinged with gold as the sun began to slip behind the hill. Ham LaFontaine was driving, she saw, his beefy, sunburned arm resting on the open window frame, his cap pulled low on his forehead. Behind him, on the passenger side, she could just make out her father's upright figure. Amber felt the air rush out of her as if she'd been holding her breath since she first heard the truck. Her father was back. Not hurt and not caught. The truck stopped with a grinding of brakes only a foot or so from where Amber stood, its back wheels skidding slightly sideways.

"Scared ya!" Ham said, and spit tobacco juice out the window near her feet.

"Didn't see me flinch!" she said.

He shook his head and grinned, his teeth stained

with dark juice. "Nah, you're pretty good."

Charles Landis opened the truck's other door and stepped out. When he left, he'd been wearing a business suit, but now he was dressed like the other men in camouflage. Amber did her best to keep her expression as impassive as Cassie's, as if this was just an ordinary homecoming. Her father didn't know she knew what they'd been doing or how serious it was.

Her father nodded at the three of them and then turned back to the truck, to get something out of the cab.

The other men were climbing down from the back of the truck now. Mack Sturdivant and Virgil Conway, followed by Duane Bruder and the O'Donnell brothers. She didn't know how many men had been involved in the mission altogether, but these were the Cadre, the men her father trusted. Most of all, he trusted Mack, his second-in-command, who'd had guerrilla training in Central America and the Middle East. Mack, strategist and explosives expert, would have led the mission.

"Cassie!" her father called. "Is that old mattress still down in the basement?"

"Sure. What do you want it for?"

"Duane and Virgil, you boys go down and bring it up to the toolshed. Cassie, dig up a sleeping bag and bring it out here." The three people who'd been given their orders moved hurriedly to carry them out. Charles Landis backed around the open door of the truck, and Amber saw what he'd been retrieving. It was a kid, a black kid, asleep or unconscious, as far as she could tell. His head hung down, and his legs and one arm dangled limply in her father's arms. Was it somebody hurt in the bombing? Or was it maybe the kid the news story had talked about? The kid who'd escaped from the mental institution?

Her father turned to her, then, blue eyes vibrant in his tanned, lined face. "Amber, you go inside and fix this kid a sandwich or something. He hasn't eaten in who knows how long."

She couldn't ask if it was the crazy kid, of course. She wasn't supposed to know about him.

Charles Landis took the boy to the toolshed that leaned at an odd angle against the barn, and kicked open the door. "Kenny, go find me a padlock."

"Yes, sir!" Kenny said, and pushed the other cookie into his mouth as he headed into the house.

"Amber, what're you waiting for? Get this kid some food!"

As Amber turned to go, a huge bird drifted down and landed on the roof of the barn. It seemed to come out of nowhere, like a shadow appearing as the sun sank lower in the sky. Inky black, it looked like a crow, but bigger. Much bigger. It ruffled its wings a couple of times and then stood, looking down, its attention fixed on her father as he stepped into the shed with the boy in his arms. It opened and shut its heavy black beak but made no sound. Amber rubbed at the back of her neck, where she'd felt a sudden chill. And then went inside to get something for the kid to eat.

Amber sat cross-legged on the floor of the shed next to the stained mattress that took up most of the available floor space. The plate she had brought out with its peanut butter and jelly sandwich tilted slightly where one side rested on the edge of the tattered sleeping bag and the other on the mattress itself. Droplets of water had run down the can of cold soda and made a little puddle on the floor. The boy had not moved since she set the can and plate down for him and told him she'd brought him supper.

She wanted to be in the house right now. Her father might be telling Cassie about the mission, explaining what had really happened, what they had done, what they were going to do now. Kenny was in there. He hadn't been sent out on some stupid errand to make this kid eat. Maybe she could just leave the food. It wasn't her fault if he didn't have the sense to wake up and eat it. Her father couldn't very well blame her for what some crazy kid did or didn't do. But as much as she wanted to go back to the house, she didn't get up. For a reason she couldn't explain to herself, she just sat there, looking at the kid.

He was lying on his side on top of the open sleeping bag, his eyes closed, both clenched fists beneath his chin and his knees pulled up almost far enough to meet those tight fists. His chest moved only slightly as he breathed. The light from the fluorescent camping lantern shone on his dark skin and hair, on his striped shirt and the jeans with the frayed hems, and glinted off the metal bracelet lying on the floor next to the mattress. It had been around the boy's ankle before her father had cut it off with tin snips. The thing, her father said, that was meant to keep kids at the hospital from running away. This one hadn't worked.

It was still warm in the shed, warmer than it was outside, now that the sun had gone down and the twilight mountain chill had begun. "If you don't eat, you'll starve, you know," she said to the unmoving figure.

As she said it, a memory suddenly rose in her mind. Baby rabbits. She'd found them, two of them, in a shallow, fur-lined hole in the ground in the backyard of one of the apartments they'd had in Plattsburgh. It was an old, old memory, but so clear now that Amber felt almost as if she'd slipped back in time, as if she was six years old again, picking the rabbits up from their nest. They had been tiny, smaller than her fist, their eyes not open yet. She could almost feel again their hearts beating fast under her fingers, their tiny ears like velvet against her cheek when she held them close.

She had put them in a shoe box lined with one of Kenny's old frayed diapers, taken it inside, and hidden it under her bed. She had wanted the rabbits to be hers. Only hers. She didn't want Kenny even to know about them. She wouldn't have trusted Kenny with them. Not since the bad time. That was when he'd started being mean. Little as he was, his meanness had begun to scare her sometimes.

She'd gone to the refrigerator and gotten some lettuce to feed them. She wanted to give them a carrot—she knew rabbits ate carrots—but there weren't any in the vegetable drawer. So she made do with lettuce, which she put into the shoe box along with a saucerful of water for them to drink.

But they hadn't eaten the lettuce. The next morning she couldn't even tell if they had drunk any of the water, because it was all spilled. The rabbits were curled up in one corner of the box, their fur dark and wet.

All that day, whenever she could get away from Kenny and the baby-sitter, she had tried to get the rabbits to eat the lettuce. She tore it into little pieces that didn't look too big for their tiny mouths. But they wouldn't open their mouths any more than they would open their eyes. Finally she tried forcing their mouths open, forcing the lettuce in, all the time telling them,

"Chew, bunnies, chew it up. You got to eat!" She had felt like crying about their not eating.

She *hadn't*, though. It was the first summer after the bad time, the summer her father had started being away all the time, leaving them with people they didn't know. She had cried about it the first time, and her father had told her about the war he was fighting. He'd made her and Kenny promise to be his very best soldiers. Soldiers, he told them, didn't cry. Not ever.

The next morning she'd waited till Kenny had gotten up to go to the bathroom before she pulled the shoe box out from under the bed. The baby rabbits were dead. They were cold and stiff, their still-wet fur all matted and clumped. She didn't cry then either. She had wanted to bury them in the backyard, but she couldn't remember now what had happened to them. The memory seemed to end there: pulling the box out, finding them dead. There were lots of things she didn't remember from that summer.

Amber shook herself a little, bringing herself back to the present, to the warm shed and the crazy little boy. She reached out one finger and gingerly poked him. Elijah, her father had said his name was. It was just about all he had said about him. Nothing about a search for him. But then he hadn't talked about the other search yet either or about the bombing.

"Elijah," she said now, and shook the boy a little. There was no response. "Elijah. Wake up. You have to eat something!"

Amber couldn't remember the word the news bulletin had used, the kind of crazy he was. She wondered if he was dangerous in some way. But he didn't look dangerous. No more dangerous than the rabbits. "Elijah!" she said again, louder. She thought she saw his eyelids flutter a little at the sound of his name. "You gotta eat!"

Elijah lay very still, his eyes closed. A pain in his stomach reminded him that he was hungry, more than hungry. It was hunger that had melted his intention to keep himself stone. He did not know where he was. But wherever he was, it was quiet. The roar of violence had faded. The air here was hot and still. He smelled the musty smell of the sleeping bag beneath his cheek and felt a trickle of sweat sliding down his neck.

A tiny sound, like breath, told him he was not alone. Unmoving, he sensed outward. Whoever was here did not seem to be a threat. But that didn't make him safe, he knew. Whoever was here was related in some way to the others, the men with big hands and hard shoulders who brought the roar of violence and the white-haired man with the wolf tattoo and the icy cold eyes.

"Elijah." The voice was a girl's voice, like honey on burned toast. Soft and sweet over something crisped with fire. "You gotta eat!"

He did his best to ignore the voice, but his stomach responded on its own, rumbling again so that he knew the person who had spoken must have heard. He could smell the unmistakable scent of peanut butter now and longed to respond. Instead he squeezed his eyes more tightly.

He felt the marble in his hand, imagined the look of it, the blue and white swirl in its center like the earth, as his great-grandmother had said when she gave it to him. "We're all in that little ball together," she had told him, "looking up and out at the hand of God." He wanted to take himself into that blue and white center. But he couldn't keep the image of the marble clear in his mind. It blinked out, and in its place came another. It was a cardboard box with a wet, frayed white cloth folded inside. Huddled in the corner were a pair of baby rabbits. Dead.

With that image came an overpowering sense of loss he knew all too well. It was like his own. Like the loss of everyone who had ever mattered in his life. No!

"You gotta eat!" The voice came again. He opened his eyes and found himself looking into the face of a girl with long, straight blond hair. He closed his eyes again, gripping the marble in his right hand more tightly, trying to think his way into it, or into the mountain, anywhere away from this girl.

"I brought you some supper."

It was too late. The rabbits had been her rabbits, he

HIGH FRONTIER
SCHOOL LIBRARY

knew. But the loss was deeper than any rabbit babies, as deep in her as in himself. A connection had been made between them. Whether he wanted it or not made no difference.

"You gotta eat!" she said.

Elijah pulled the sleeping bag up over his shoulder and huddled into the musty mattress. The girl, who had not spoken to him again, had taken away the plate as soon as he'd finished eating. The heat of the day was long gone, and he was cold. He had not been able to shut himself down, turn himself to stone. Not since the baby rabbits had wakened the ache for all that was gone from him now.

He held his marble up in front of his face. But it was too dark to see it. He yawned. He would have liked to sleep, but he was afraid sleep might make things worse. He didn't want to dream again. Dreams had connected him to the others like himself, the new kids, the Ark kids. Dreams had given them their quest. And a dream had shown him that the quest had ended when the Ark family was torn apart.

He had run away not just to hide but to die. Elijah knew about death. Mama Effie, his great-grandmother, had died. His mother had died, beaten to death by the man who had first brought the roar of violence into Elijah's world. Death was an ending. Once and forever.

The idea didn't frighten him. There were other things that frightened him far more.

But his plan hadn't worked. He was still alive, and the frightening things still existed in the world outside his skin.

He felt himself sliding toward sleep and tried to blink, to squeeze the marble tight enough to keep himself there in the shed with the smell of mildew and dust and old motor oil. The warmth of the sleeping bag lulled him, and he thought of kicking it off, but he was too tired to move. Images began swirling together, then melted into darkness.

And he was flying. As in all the other dreams, he was a raven, his shiny black wings holding him steady in the air. This time, as last time, he was alone. Above him stretched the endless reaches of sky, blue and empty. Beneath was a vast expanse of blackened plain stretching toward a range of mountains that rose to pale, snow-covered peaks at the edges of the sky.

He flew onward, feeling his loneliness like an arrow in his heart, and gradually the burned land gave way to low, grassy hills dusted with snow. Bare, leafless trees grew singly or in clusters, their branches casting stark shadows on the pale ground. Still there was no sign of life below him. He moved his wings more slowly now, feeling a current of air beneath him, lifting him toward the mountains that lay ahead. On their slopes the trees, most of them evergreens, grew thickly, humped beneath a thick covering of snow.

There was something down there in the winter mountain's forest, something dark he could not see, that seemed to pull at him, dragging him down out of the sky. He fought, flapping his strong wings more powerfully, angling himself upward toward the light. But little by little the forest below him came closer.

Elijah woke, shivering. He was lying on the mattress, the sleeping bag tangled around his legs. He reached to pull it up and realized that both hands were empty. He groped frantically until he found the hard, cool roundness of his marble, and then he held it for a moment against his cheek.

Knock.

The sound came from the shed door.

Knock.

Elijah would have liked to burrow into the sleeping bag, curl himself into a ball, slip into the quiet safety of the marble, but the sound at the door lured him. What could be making it? He sensed outward and found nothing that he recognized. No sense of a person nearby. Clutching his marble tightly in one hand, he moved to the door. He remembered the sharp click of a padlock snapping into place after the girl had left. He couldn't simply open the door and look out. Pale silvery light came through cracks between the boards of the door from the moonlit night outside. *Knock*.

Elijah pressed an eye to one of the cracks. He could see a tuft of grass and a narrow slice of the packed dirt driveway beyond. Into that space moved a black shape. It was as familiar to him as his dream. A raven. It moved toward him and struck the wood of the door with its heavy beak. *Knock*. The bird tipped its head then, its eye catching a gleam of moonlight. For a moment the two of them were still, regarding each other in the darkness.

Elijah's memory jumped back to when Mama Effie and he had sat on the front porch of their little house in North Carolina and read together the Bible story of Noah and the Ark. He had been a little boy in diapers then, a little boy nobody but his great-grandmother knew was reading already, a little boy who knew things nobody that little was supposed to know.

"You remember the raven," Mama Effie had said when they'd finished the story. "Everybody knows about the dove bringing back the olive branch. Don't nobody remember that Noah sent the raven first. That bird, it never came back. It just kept on flying out over the water that covered the world. Weeks it flew, day and night, till the water went down and land appeared." Mama Effie's voice had been full of the wonder of it. "Some bird, that raven. Some black survivor of a bird."

Elijah looked into the eye of the raven now, the tiny

white circle of moon reflected in it.

Live. Elijah knew just as surely as if the bird had spoken the word, that he was meant to live, not to die. No matter how frightening the world he found himself in.

The raven stepped back from the door and with a flap of its massive wings rose out of sight. Elijah shivered. He knew something else. It would do no good to try to escape from his dreams. Long ago Elijah had found a way to close off his eyes, shut down his ears, turn himself inward away from the painful and terrifying world. It's what had sent him to Laurel Mountain. But dreams were different. He had never succeeded in turning them off. He knew the reason now. To live, he needed to dream.

DAY TWO

Amber jerked open another drawer in the warped and peeling dresser that held her meager supply of clothes, scooped the contents out, and dumped them on her bed. *The* bed. It had never really been hers, this room with its bed and dresser, the little closet with the slanted ceiling tucked under the eaves, the narrow window from which she could just see the grassy edge of the pond through the leaves of the silver maple. The pale gray light of dawn came through that window now.

She wouldn't mind leaving this place she had pretended for a while was home, if it meant she could *do* something. All her life, even after Cassie had come to live with them, she'd been moved from one place to another. It was how things went in a war. But now that the war had turned hot, really hot for the first time ever, her father was telling her she was just a child. A child with nothing useful to offer, who had to run away and hide.

A safe place Cassie was taking them to, Amber and Kenny and the hostage kid—Elijah. A place Amber had never heard of even though her father had bought it ages ago for just such a time as this. Another thing it had been better for her not to know. And now nobody would say how long they would have to stay there, how long they had to hide. All they would say was that she was allowed to take only what would fit in a canoe.

Amber picked up the red three-ring binder from her bookshelf and leafed through it. Her father had promised her she could take over the kid page on the Militia's netsite soon, and she'd written a lot of stuff for it. Stuff she was proud of. It wasn't just war games and military strategies that were needed to realize her father's vision. The biggest part of the fight was the fight for people's minds. So he wrote and spoke and helped people understand what was going wrong in the world. And how it could be fixed. It was what *she* wanted to do too, what she was getting really good at doing. Except that only she and Cassie knew it. Her father hadn't even taken the time to read it yet, much less let it go up on the netsite.

She turned to the essay she'd written about her father, "Charles Landis, Alpha Wolf and American Hero." This was a man, Amber had written, who stood for freedom, not just for people, but for the planet. A man who knew that government, this one or any other, was all about greed and self-interest and the struggle for power. If people—all men, all women, all children—were to be truly free, then governments had to go. Governments let a few people get rich and powerful while everybody else was kept poor and weak. They used up the resources of the earth and polluted everything with toxic waste. Charles Landis was the man who could show people how to change that.

The leader of a wolf pack was the strongest and most intelligent individual, the alpha male. Charles Landis, with the head of a wolf tattooed on the back of his right hand, was that kind of leader. The alpha wolf. He was the man who would lead North America into the new millennium and make a world where all the mistakes of the old one could be corrected.

Amber closed the notebook and put it back on the shelf. She didn't have to take it to the safe place. The essay, and everything else she'd written, were in the computer in the basement and would go with her father when he took whatever couldn't be left here for the authorities to find when they came. He'd promised, she assured herself. As soon as they could come out of hiding, she'd get to take over the kid page. He'd promised.

She sighed. Whatever her father ordered, she would do, just like everybody else. Like always. And if, for now, it meant running away, hiding, then she would run and hide.

She opened her duffel bag, jammed in her clothes,

and zipped it. As she dropped the bag on the floor, the door banged open, and Kenny barged in, dressed in a ragged T-shirt and camouflage pants, multiple pockets bulging, a backpack on his back.

"You aren't allowed in my room," Amber said automatically.

"It isn't yours anymore," Kenny said. "Aren't you ready yet?"

She pulled the blanket off her bed and began folding it, not answering.

Kenny went to the window and looked out. "The truck's nearly packed. Did you see it? Ham went and traded the other one for it during the night. It's a bread truck. They won't stop a bread truck. Dad's taking everything over to Plattsburgh."

She took the sheets off the bed as well. She heard the distant *thump-thump* of a helicopter.

"Even if a chopper goes right over our heads, there wouldn't be anything to see. Almost all the guys are gone." Kenny went to the door and turned back, holding the doorknob. "Hurry up. Cassie wants you to help her with that crazy kid."

When Kenny left, Amber took the sheets from the bed and rolled them, along with her blanket, into a tight bedroll with her favorite squishy pillow in the center.

There was a knock at her open door, and her father stuck his head in.

"You ready?"

Amber nodded.

Charles Landis, dressed now in faded blue jeans and a plaid shirt with its sleeves rolled up, took two steps into the room. Even dressed as he was, he carried himself like a leader, someone who was used to being in command. He looked around and nodded. "Duane'll take care of the rest of your things."

Amber looked up at him. Movie star handsome he was, with his thick white hair, his tanned face and intensely blue eyes. He was old enough to be her grandfather, but nothing about him seemed old. He was more energetic than Ham, smarter *and* stronger than Virgil or Duane. You could feel the power that radiated from him. It was no wonder people did what he wanted them to do. "What are you going to do now?" she asked.

"Stay out in the open. The way I did Wednesday, speaking at the fund-raiser right under their noses at the same time as the bombing. I'll be where the media can find me and the feds can keep me under surveillance. Or think they're keeping me under surveillance. Letting them see we've got nothing to hide."

"What about the fax that said we did it?"

"Part of a bigger plan. I've already denied that. When they find me, later today, I'll deny it again. To the media too. There's never been a word in all my published writing about terrorism. I've never once advocated bombing bridges."

Amber thought of the news bulletin she wasn't supposed to have read. "People died in the bombing, didn't they?"

Charles Landis answered without a pause. "Necessary losses."

Amber became aware, suddenly, of her heart beating in her chest. A flash of something, an image, a memory maybe, flew through her mind, but it was gone before she could catch it, leaving only a shadow of pain.

"People die in war," her father said, dismissing the subject with a wave of his hand.

"How many died on the highway?" The number was burned into her brain. One hundred and eighty-three.

"It doesn't matter." She looked up into the blue intensity of his eyes as he took hold of her shoulders, his hands warm through her T-shirt. "Listen to me, Amber. People die every day. They die in cars and planes. Fall out of canoes and drown. Get sick. People die stupid, meaningless deaths." He closed his eyes a moment, barely longer than a blink, his forehead creased. "These deaths weren't meaningless. What is at stake here is so big, so important that those few insignificant lives have taken on a whole new meaning."

She nodded.

He released her then. "Cassie's waiting for you," he said as he turned to go. "Better get on down."

A light head wind ruffled the surface of the water, so that moving the canoes, loaded with packs, tarps, bedrolls, coolers and bags of food, dishes, utensils, fishing gear, and extra paddles, took more effort than Kenny was used to. In the bow of the smaller canoe as they crossed the pond, he dug his paddle deeply into the water, two strokes on the right, two strokes on the left, changing hands to keep the strain on his arms carefully balanced. Ham had warned him about letting his right-handedness result in a weak left arm. In hand-to-hand combat it was important not to give an opponent any weakness to exploit. Kenny didn't care what his stroking pattern did to the movement of the canoe. It was Amber, in the stern, who had to worry about steering.

Kenny thought of the deer rifle and shotgun at the bottom of the canoe, beneath the other gear. They, and the deer rifle in Cassie's canoe, would be the only guns where they were going. No more target practice with the AK-47s and Tech-9s the guys had been teaching him to use. He'd complained about this while they were loading the boats, but Cassie told him that rifles and shotguns were a lot easier for a woman and three children to explain, if it came to explaining, than military weapons.

Kenny dug his paddle deeper, grunting with the effort. *Three* children. He couldn't see why they had to bring the crazy black kid along. If military weapons, hidden at the bottoms of the boats, could give them problems, what did they think having the stupid hostage along was going to do? The feds were supposed to be looking for him at the same time they looked for the bombers, so having him with them was practically like putting up a sign. How many crazy black kids did they think were loose in the Adirondacks at any given time?

He looked over at Cassie's canoe, where the boy was huddled in the bow, eyes shut, curled into himself against a pack filled with clothes—*Kenny's* clothes—jeans and shorts and shirts that Cassie had said the kid could have because Kenny had outgrown them. Nobody had asked *him* if he wanted to give them away.

The kid was dangerous, Kenny thought. Not just because he made them conspicuous. What if he got away and talked? Cassie said he couldn't talk, but what if she was wrong? *Autistic* she said he was. Brain-damaged. Or crazy. It didn't matter which. It was stupid to take him with them. It was no good arguing, of course. An order was an order. But Kenny didn't have to like it.

He paddled hard on the left, and the canoe veered

toward the right before Amber could balance his stroke. Kenny grinned to himself and flipped his paddle to splash his sister as he switched hands. Amber was stronger than he was right now, as she proved every time he challenged her to arm wrestle, but he was gaining on her fast. One of these days he was going to pass her. Their father said it was inevitable. He might not ever be able to catch up in age, but he was a boy, and that meant he'd be stronger than she was. Soon, probably, and then forever. He put his back into his paddling and pictured his muscles getting stronger with every stroke. Things would be different from now on, their father had said. When this war turned into a real shooting war, Kenny Landis was going to be ready.

Cassie's larger, heavier canoe was staying even with theirs, even though she was paddling alone. "Where are we going?" Amber asked her now. Their father had refused to say.

"Deep in," Cassie answered. "Three ponds, one lake, and a river."

"How long will it take?"

Cassie scanned the hazy white sky. "If the weather holds, two days."

"Why can't we go by truck?" Kenny asked.

"There's no open road in."

"If there's no road," Amber asked, "what's there?"

"It's an old summer camp, abandoned since the fifties. Called Paradise Park."

Kenny stopped paddling, so that Cassie's boat moved ahead. "Paradise? I've heard Mack talk about that sometimes. I thought it was code."

"Paddle!" Amber said. "I'm not doing this for two days all by myself!"

"Has Dad been using this place for long? What's he been using it for?"

But Cassie would say no more about their destination.

Need to know, Kenny thought. It meant that nobody was told anything they didn't absolutely have to know until they absolutely had to know it. So that if they were caught, they would have as little information as possible for the cops or the feds to beat out of them. There were lots of things even Cassie didn't know. Kenny didn't mind as much as Amber did about not knowing stuff. They were guerrilla fighters. That's just how it had to be.

But he hated having to hide. It seemed to him the Militia had plenty of weapons and they ought to use them. The bombing had been a good start. It was the biggest terrorist attack ever in the United States. So why weren't they going to keep it up? Right now, before the system could recover, they ought to go after power stations and water supplies and the state buildings in

Albany maybe, stuff he'd heard Mack talking about. Really fight the war Charles Landis was always talking about. Bring the whole system down once and for all. Kenny wished they were a real army, with tanks and planes and rockets and enough men to just take over the government and make things work the way they wanted them to work. Right now.

Then nobody would have to hide in the woods like an animal.

They were hiding, their father said, because they were valuable, he and Amber—the only children of the leader of the Free Mountain Militia. The cops and feds would come after the two of them if they could. And if they found them, they'd use them as leverage against him. To get him to talk. He and Amber would be hostages then. And in hostage situations people could die. Their lives—and maybe the Militia itself—depended on how thoroughly they could disappear.

So here they were, Charles Landis's valuable family, paddling to Paradise to disappear—his half-breed Indian wife, his two blond kids, and the one who wasn't family, wasn't valuable, this crazy black kid who didn't talk and hardly ever even opened his eyes.

A shadow swept over the water, and Kenny looked up to see a raven winging its way over their heads toward the mass of cattails where the portage trail began that led to the next pond. The bird dipped low over the reeds and then rose toward the trees beyond them.

Cassie stopped paddling for a moment and watched as it disappeared among the trees. She said nothing, but when she returned to paddling, her stroke seemed tighter, less smooth and easy. Cassie had gone all Indian and weird over that stupid bird. Talking as if it had some kind of meaning, hanging around them. She said Adirondack ravens didn't come near people, let alone follow them around, because people had hunted them till they were almost extinct. Kenny wished he could dig the shotgun out from under their gear. He'd make this one extinct in a minute!

DAY THREE

They had camped the night before near a small pond, pitching their two tents well up under the trees and pulling the canoes out of the water to keep them from being visible from the air. Amber had had to share one tent with Kenny, while Cassie and Elijah took the other. At first light Cassie had wakened them, handing them their breakfast—peanut butter on bread and cups of Tang—and urging them to get their shoes on and their gear packed.

In less than half an hour they'd been on their way, portaging the canoes to the next pond and then returning to carry their gear. Each portage required several trips, Kenny complaining steadily that Elijah not only didn't have to do any of the work but made more work for the rest of them. "Just be glad you aren't the one who has to carry him," Cassie had told him.

"How much farther do we have to go?" Kenny asked now, as they paddled along the river that was to be the last part of the water highway they were taking to Paradise Park. All morning clouds had hidden the sun and seemed to threaten rain, but by early afternoon the sun had come out. It was high and hot now, and all three of them were sweating as they paddled.

"Not far," Cassie said. It had been her steady answer since they had stopped for a quick lunch of hard-boiled eggs and nectarines.

"What's *far*?" Kenny asked. "Alaska?"

"We'll take the canoes out about a mile upriver from here. The last part we do on foot." Kenny groaned. "Unless you'd just like to go back where we came from and let the feds take you hostage." Cassie shielded her eyes from the sun and scanned the sky over her head.

Amber looked up, trying to see what Cassie was looking for. After a moment she saw it, the high dark speck that was the raven. They had not seen it at their campsite the night before, but they had heard it nearby, its hoarse call sounding from the tops of trees not far away. It was weird, this bird following them. More than weird. Unless it went out hunting at night like an owl, the bird couldn't have eaten since it had appeared with the truck that brought Elijah. It had flown over them first thing this morning as they pushed their reloaded canoes away from shore, and flown with them all day. Now it was circling on thermals high above them.

"Do you think the raven has something to do with Elijah?" Amber asked.

Kenny snorted and sent a splash toward her again at the end of his paddle stroke. "Oh, sure. The bird is the kid's guardian angel. I ought to shoot the thing the next time it comes close enough. Big, ugly crow."

"Ravens are protected," Cassie said.

"Since when do *we* care about laws?" Kenny said.

"Who said anything about laws?" Cassie paddled more quickly then, moving her canoe in front of theirs. Amber looked at the stock of the shotgun sticking out from beneath a backpack near her feet and wondered whether the raven had sense enough to stay out of range.

By the time Cassie headed her canoe toward the river's edge where a sandbank studded with flat rocks made a wide, semicircular beach between two overhanging bushes, Amber's arms and shoulders ached and there were blisters on both her palms. What she wanted to do when they landed was to flop down on the sand and let the water run over her hot, sweaty body. She hoped Cassie would let them rest awhile before they began the overland trek to the camp. No telling how far they would have to lug their stuff. She steered for the water's edge and felt the current's pressure fall off as the canoe slipped into the protected water of the river bend.

Suddenly from far above them came a harsh, raucous cry unlike anything Amber had ever heard. It was repeated once, twice, a third time. Cassie, who had just beached her canoe against the bank, looked up, and Amber followed the line of her gaze. The raven was plummeting down from the sky at tremendous speed, calling—shrieking—as it came. It sped downward, growing larger and larger, and landed with a flurry of wings on a high branch of a white pine well back from the river. There it shifted its weight from foot to foot and shrieked again.

"Quick!" Cassie said, her voice urgent. "Get your canoe up and out of the water as fast as you can." She leaped from her boat and splashed through the shallow water to grab the bowline and pull it up the beach. Amber and Kenny did as she'd said, beaching their boat as quickly as they could and jumping out to pull it after hers.

"What's up?" Kenny asked as they dragged at their canoe, its hull scraping over the sand and rocks of the riverbank. "What's the hurry?"

Cassie bent and lifted Elijah out of his place, balanced him against one hip, and pulled his bag out as well. She set the bag on the dry sand and put Elijah down on top of it before she answered. "I don't know. But I recognize a warning when I hear one. We've got to get the boats out of sight and ourselves out of here—now!"

Working as fast as they could, they dragged the canoes up under the bushes, pulled reeds from the shallows, and added them to the cover the leaves made, till there was nothing to be seen except varied shades of green where the boats were hidden. "Now run!" Cassie said, pointing up over the steep edge of the riverbank toward the distant line of trees that marked the edge of forestland. "There's not enough cover here. We've got to get in under the trees."

Now there was no need to ask what the hurry was. They could hear the distant *thump-thump* of helicopter blades. They began to run, tall grasses, slender saplings, and the thorns of berry bushes slashing at their arms and legs as they plunged through the dense greenery. Elijah, who had been as limp as a rag doll when she took him from the canoe, now clung to Cassie, arms around her neck and legs around her waist as she ran.

Amber could feel her heart thudding in her throat and ears as the sound of the helicopter grew steadily louder. She dared not look back over her shoulder to see if the chopper had risen over the ridge behind them, was close enough to see them. Until this minute, she realized, nothing that had happened since she read that news bulletin had seemed entirely real to her. Not the mission, the bombing, the deaths. Not even the need to go into hiding. It had all seemed like some kind of story the adults had created. Like the war games the Militia played for training. But this was no game.

Ahead of her, Kenny had reached the line of trees. She was only a few steps behind, nearly under cover herself, when she tripped on a bramble and went down hard on a rock, wrenching her knee and tearing her left arm from wrist to elbow on a jagged stick. Cassie, immediately behind her, nearly went down with her but caught herself in time and dodged sideways and around. As Amber tried to catch her breath, fighting the wave of pain that roared up from her knee, Cassie pushed Kenny down to lie flat behind the line of heavy undergrowth that edged the forest. She settled Elijah nearby and then ran back to drag Amber up and after them.

Thump-thump, thump-thump, thump-thump.

The sound pounded down at them as the helicopter rose into sight over the nearest ridge and then began to follow the river's course across the open land, flying low over the water. Her knee throbbing and the gash on her arm burning like a flame, Amber lay in the leaf and pine needle litter next to Elijah and looked up between the feathery green branches of a cedar sapling to watch the ominous, insectlike craft pound its way past them and on up the now-empty riverbed.

When at last the sound faded, Cassie sat up. "We wait awhile here now, in case it comes back."

Kenny sat up, brushing twigs and leaves from his T-shirt. "If I'd just had one of the guns—"

"You'd have shown them where we were," Cassie finished. "Amber, you okay?"

Amber shook her head. Blood was dripping down her arm, and her knee had begun to swell already, the skin turning a dull, mean-looking blue.

"There's a first-aid kit at the camp. There's one in my pack too, but I want to be sure they're not coming back before I go out to the canoe." She took Amber's arm and looked carefully at the gash. "This is deep. We need to clean it out. And get a cold pack on your knee. Kenny, you and I will have to go on into the camp. We'll make sure things are all right there and bring back what we need. Amber's not going to do much walking with that knee. It's going to take us longer to get our stuff to the camp now."

"Duh!" Kenny's pale eyes rested on Amber's arm. "You'd think the least you could do is stay on your feet!"

"It could have happened to any of us," Cassie told him. "Now get up off your butt, and let's go. The sooner we get there, the sooner we get back and get Amber's cut attended to. I don't want to have to deal with an infection on top of everything else."

"Can't we at least get some stuff to carry in so this won't be a wasted trip?"

"If we could take the chance of going out and unloading the canoes, we wouldn't need to go looking for the other first-aid kit, now would we?" Cassie stood. "You two will be okay here?"

Amber nodded. "We aren't going anywhere."

"Duh!" Kenny said again.

"How'd you know the raven was warning us?"

Cassie shrugged.

"And how'd the raven—"

Cassie shook her head. "No point asking questions we don't have answers for." She stood still for a moment, as if getting her bearings, and then started off through the trees. "Let's go, Kenny. The sooner we get there, the sooner we get back."

"Where's the trail?" Kenny asked as he followed her.

"In my head," Cassie answered.

When they had gone, Elijah, who was still lying on his stomach where Cassie had put him, pushed himself up into a kneeling position. He opened the fist that he kept clenched so tightly. In his palm was a large clear glass marble with a swirl of blue and white in the center. He looked at it a moment and then shoved it into the pocket of his jeans. Then he looked at Amber, his dark eyes focused and intense.

"What?" she asked, feeling an impulse to back away. She felt as if she was made of glass, like his marble, and he was seeing clear through her.

After a moment he sat, crossing his legs under him,

leaned toward her, and placed both his hands on her swollen, discolored knee. She jerked, expecting pain, but his touch was so light she could barely feel it. He stayed that way, very still, looking down at his hands, and then he closed his eyes and sat as if listening to something, his hands resting gently on the darkening bruise. After a moment she felt her knee getting warm and a vibrating sensation so slight she thought at first that she must be imagining it.

For a long time they sat that way, neither moving, heat growing steadily under Elijah's hands. Suddenly the ache in her knee flared up, becoming a sharp, fiery intensity. Amber started to pull away, but before she could move, the pain sputtered like a dying candle flame and flickered out. She blinked. The pain was gone. Completely, totally gone.

As she realized that, she became aware of her arm, blood still dripping slowly from the wound, the ragged edge of pain welling up there now.

"Can you do that to my arm too?" she asked. "Whatever it was you just did?"

Elijah moved his head so slightly she couldn't tell whether he was nodding or shaking it or whether he was responding to her question at all. He turned away from her and dragged the marble back out of his pocket. He set it on the flat of his outstretched palm, held it in a shaft of sunlight coming through the cedar branches, and set it spinning with his other hand.

From above them came a soft *quork*, and she looked up to see the raven, ruffling its feathers on a branch of a yellow birch tree, as if it had materialized there.

Amber cradled her arm and hoped Cassie would be back very soon.

After the woman with the long black braid had put him down, Elijah had lain still, listening to the helicopter overhead. As loud as that sound was, it came from outside, through his ears. It was something he heard the way other people hear, not something that rose inside his own mind, like the growl that meant menace and danger, violence simmering beneath the surface of things. Or the roar that meant the unleashing of it. The men they had come away from had made the roar louder in Elijah's head than he had ever known it. But there had been no such roar from the helicopter. It brought only the mechanical sound of engine and rotors.

Whatever these people feared from the helicopter, whatever threat made the raven scream and the people run and hide, it was not the sort of danger the roar warned of. The men above would not have sent death down on them from the sky.

He did not understand what these people intended to do with him. They had taken him out of the shed with the padlocked door, but he was no more free now than he had been at Laurel Mountain. There the bracelet on his ankle had kept him prisoner, till he used the hospital's computer to shut off the alarms and ran away. Here, without locks or bracelet or alarms, he was still captive. He did not know where he was, where or how to run. When the raven came to him, he had known that his job was to live. To do that, he must stay for now with these people. There was no other way.

As the helicopter sound faded into the distance, he had heard the woman speaking to the girl, Amber. When she had fallen, he knew instantly that she was hurt. He had known it the way he always knew when Mama Effie was hurting in the night, the way Mama Effie had known to come and gentle him when his dreams were bad, even before he had wakened enough to call out. Connection.

He had also understood from the moment the girl had hurt herself that he could help. He had not thought to question it. He leaned forward and put his hands on Amber's knee. He held them still, as the dream memory of Taryn's healings rose in his mind and showed him what to do. He felt a kind of pulsing throb beneath the girl's swollen, discolored skin. Taking slow, deep breaths, concentrating on stillness, he let light and warmth flow through his hands.

When the heat left his hands, he sat back. Amber was saying something to him, but he refused to listen. The ache in his heart was unbearable. Taryn, the girl who could heal, who had taught the other Ark kids to reach their minds into trees and rocks and mountains, was lost to him now. As were the others. The connections had been broken. As connections always broke. Always. He did not want this Amber, daughter of the cold-eyed man, alive in the vast, empty darkness inside himself. He dug into his pocket and retrieved his marble. Setting it spinning, he lost himself in its blue and white depths.

Pop! At first she thought it was a firecracker in the darkness. Until she heard Cassie scream. Pop! Another firecracker sound and another. The car skidded to a stop, throwing Amber against her shoulder belt. There were people in front of the car now, men in uniforms lit up by the headlights. Men carrying guns. There was shouting from outside. And inside the car Cassie yelling, "No, no, no!" as she struggled to release her seat belt, as she pushed the car door open, tried to get out.

Men in uniforms surrounded the car, shoved Cassie back inside, leveled their guns at the car windows. Amber tried to see ahead of them on the road, tried to see the red pickup truck her mother was in. But all she could see were the men. Beside her, strapped into his car seat, Kenny was crying. A confusion of voices. Moving shadows, flashlights, guns. And a feeling in Amber's stomach, as if she'd been kicked. "Where's Mama?" Amber asked Cassie, who was beating on the steering wheel with both fists. "What's happened? Where's Mama?"

Amber woke, tears caught in her throat. It was the first time she'd had that old dream in years. She knew what had brought it back. The feeling as she'd lain flat on the ground, watching the helicopter through the cedar branches. Fear of the men in uniforms. It was an old dream. After all this time she could not sort out which images and sounds had been burned into her mind the night her mother died and which had been invented in the recurring nightmare she'd had for months, maybe years afterward. The nightmare that had come back tonight in all its original horror.

She lay on the bed that was little more than a sleeping shelf in the attic room of the ramshackle house in Paradise Park, willing her heart to slow down, her throat to relax so she could swallow. She'd been six years old when it happened. She had heard the story told over and over since then so that she knew it by heart.

It had been a peaceful protest, her father and four other WDT men demanding that the state stop work on the highway exit that would make it easier for tourists and developers to invade the Adirondack wilderness. The men had had no weapons. They had chained themselves to the bulldozers and earthmovers to stop the work, and they had stayed there for three days without food after the police put up their barricade.

Her mother and Uncle Terrence, Cassie's husband then, had been trying to take food and water to them, trying to get the police to allow them through in the red pickup truck Terrence was driving. Cassie had been following them in her old Chevy, with Amber and Kenny in back.

There had been an argument. Afterward the police said that Terrence Landis had pulled a gun and they had shot in self-defense. Except that they had shot not just Terrence Landis, who they said had pulled the gun, but also his passenger, Marion Landis, Charles's wife, Amber and Kenny's mother. Marion Landis, who was holding a basket of sandwiches and fruit in her lap. Uncle Terrence had been killed instantly, with a bullet in the head. But Amber's mother had bled to death on the front seat of the truck while the police made no effort to call an ambulance to help her.

Self-defense. The story had been printed in the newspapers that way. Dangerous protesters, her father's group had been called. That was before her father had started the Free Mountain Militia. That was when his group had been the Wilderness Defense Team, WDT. It was true that there had been a gun in the red truck. It had not been fired. Cassie said that when at last the police let her out of the car, let her go to the truck, the gun, a .22-caliber rifle, was still on its rack in the back window. By the time reporters took their pictures, though, the gun was on the seat of the truck between the bodies of the "dangerous protesters."

The media lied. The police lied. Judges and lawyers

and the representatives of the State of New York lied. And the men in uniforms used those uniforms to kill and get away with it. She had known it, if not all her life, then since the age of six. Since the night she heard her mother shot to death and thought it was firecrackers.

There was no point thinking about it. Amber pulled her blankets up to her chin. The August heat wave was over. The night had turned cold. Her arm, anointed with antiseptic cream and wrapped in the gauze bandage Cassie had brought back, ached. Her knee was only vaguely tender to the touch.

Amber thought about what Elijah had done to her knee. It made no sense. Cassie had been surprised when Amber told her, but she had not refused to believe it, as Amber herself would have if someone had told her such a story. Started quickly enough, ice packs could keep swelling down, Amber knew, but they could not make it go immediately and entirely away once it had begun. The swelling of her knee had been gone—gone!—by the time Kenny and Cassie got back with the first-aid supplies. The bruise was still visible, but it was the only leftover from an injury that should have kept her from walking properly for days. Instead Amber had been able not just to walk to Paradise Park on her own but to carry her fair share of the supplies. Whatever it was Elijah had done, it seemed entirely impossible.

When Amber explained, though, Cassie had only looked at Elijah for a long moment and nodded. As if she had seen the sort of thing he had done before, as if in some way she had been expecting it. But she had not explained. Amber didn't understand. There was something about Elijah, something that from the moment she saw him, made him seem familiar to her. Strange. Different. But still somehow familiar. She didn't understand that either.

Amber looked up at the roof timbers above her head, just visible in the darkness. Paradise Park was a joke of a name. Work had been done on the old lodge and a couple of barns and storage sheds, but most of the buildings were falling down, roofs and walls caved in, doors off their hinges, porches sagging and full of jagged holes. Brambles were taking over everything. The only really good thing about the place was the lake. Bigger than the pond by the farmhouse, it had been created by the damming of a creek. The dam was the best-preserved piece of the property, that and the small hydroelectric plant that went with it.

"Originally the camp was self-sufficient," Cassie had told them. "They made their own electricity, grew their own vegetables, even built the buildings out of trees they cut down and turned into lumber in a sawmill by the dam." The sawmill was gone now, and there was no way even to guess where the vegetable garden might have been, though the remains of a greenhouse could be seen under a tangle of blackberry brambles. But the hydroelectric plant had been repaired, could be up and running easily. "The plan is to make the place self-sufficient again," Cassie said. "Eventually this will be the center of everything."

Some center, Amber thought. Woods and brambles and disintegrating cabins. The house they had moved into, the old caretaker's cottage, was well away from the rest of the camp. It had been built at the far end of the lake and might have been lived in for a while after the camp had quit operating. It wasn't by any stretch of the imagination a comfortably livable building yet, but Cassie said it was snug enough for now. And they would be safe here. Safe from men in uniforms who could kill whoever they wanted to kill. Amber had changed her mind. Soldier or no soldier, right now she wanted to be safe.

DAY 16

It was early afternoon when Charles Landis came out of the woods into the clearing that surrounded the old house. Mack Sturdivant, carrying a pack on his back and a high-powered rifle cradled in one arm, followed him. Kenny and Amber were swimming, Cassie watching them from the front porch. As soon as Kenny saw them, he scrambled out of the lake and came racing up, shaking water from his hair. "What's up?" he asked. "Can we go back to the farm yet?"

"You'll see."

Cassie got up, and Landis hugged her, resting his chin for a moment on the top of her head. "Have you had lunch?" she asked.

"Not unless you count a stick of jerky. I've been on the road since before dawn—drove down to Albany, then came back to Plattsburgh in a delivery truck and from there to the trailhead under the cap in the back of Duane's pickup with Mack. Officially I'm in the capital all day, meeting with lawyers. I have to get back down there tonight so I can spend the night in the hotel and drive back tomorrow."

Amber, wrapped in a towel, came up from the lakeshore.

"Where's the boy?" Landis asked.

"Out there somewhere," Cassie said waving her arm toward the woods.

"By himself? You think that's wise?"

"He doesn't go far." She led the way inside, through the empty living room and into the kitchen. "Besides, he has a kind of bodyguard."

Kenny groaned.

"Bodyguard?"

Cassie nodded at Kenny. "Go upstairs and bring down a couple of chairs," she said, "if you want to sit." Charles Landis settled into a chair at the oilcloth-covered table as Cassie rummaged in the cooler and brought out cheese and sandwich meat, set a loaf of bread on the table, and took a couple of chipped plates from a cupboard. Then she turned the flame on under the coffeepot on the camp stove. "That raven's still hanging around."

Mack shrugged off his pack, set it and the rifle in the corner, and sat at the table.

Landis regarded Cassie, his eyes narrowed. "You really think the bird has something to do with the boy."

Cassie nodded. "I know it." The men looked at each other, and Cassie shrugged. "You can believe me or not, but you asked, and I'm telling you. We've been here two weeks, and where Elijah goes, the raven goes." She leaned against the counter and folded her arms as Kenny brought in a pair of rickety wooden chairs for himself and Amber. "So . . . the message with the supply drop was that you had news. What is it?"

"Give us time to eat first," Landis said. The men made themselves sandwiches and ate them while the others waited. Finally Charles Landis wiped his mouth with a paper napkin, took a sip of coffee, and spoke. "The search is over. They got the guys who did the Northway bombing."

There was a surprised silence. Kenny looked from his father to Mack and back again. "But—but how—who?"

Landis grinned over at Cassie. "You remember Jack Lawry?"

"Of course I remember him. Ex-con and refugee from a VA mental ward. Always agitating for a shooting war. What's he been doing since you kicked him out?"

"Well, it seems he's been plotting to bomb the Northway and put the blame on me."

"But he didn't—" Kenny started.

"No, Kenny, he didn't. But it turns out there's a whole lot of evidence that says he did."

"Can't imagine how that came to be," Cassie said.

"Amazing, is what it is."

Mack laughed. "He didn't do himself any favors by filling that old cabin of his on Little Tupper Lake with guns and dynamite and blasting caps. Or hanging out with that pair of thugs he did time with in Attica. Made our job a lot easier."

"According to the federal antiterrorist task force, the three of them did the deed together," Landis said.

Mack nodded. "Terrorists, the lot of them."

"The cops and the task force and the Bureau of Alcohol, Tobacco, and Firearms surrounded his cabin, and after a couple of days he gave up. Not a shot fired, not an agent lost, you'll be pleased to know. When they searched his car, they found residue from the very explosives that were used in the bombing. They picked up the other two that night, heading for the border in a stolen car."

"The evidence is pretty strong against them too," Mack added.

Cassie nodded. "It would be, wouldn't it?" She looked at Landis. "You couldn't tell me about this?"

"Need to know."

"Right."

"I don't get it," Kenny said.

"It worked out according to plan, that's all. Jack Lawry and his buddies go to jail; I go on television and explain that he's a guy who was too sick, too violent, for us. He joined the Militia for a while, but I kicked him out, like any responsible citizen would. He's been holding a grudge against me ever since, so when he finally decided to do what we wouldn't, he sent that fax from a Kinko's and put the whole horrible thing off on us. The Militia is trained and armed only for defensive purposes. I'm just *sick* that someone would take my philosophy and turn it into a motive for terrorism." Landis leaned back in his chair, his hands clasped behind his head. "They bought the whole thing, hook, line, and sinker."

"I still don't get it," Kenny said.

"By taking credit for the bombing, we focus the world's attention on us, more attention than we've ever had before. Then, when evidence turns up showing that crazy Jack Lawry and a couple of criminal buddies of his did the bombing instead of us, we get to play the role of innocent victims. We've never had a better chance to get our message out.

"And Lawry's arrest is good for the other side too. Law enforcement looks bad when they don't solve a case as big as this. The longer they go without arresting somebody, the more upset people get. Everybody in America's been talking about the bombing, speculating, running their mouths as usual without a shred of real information. There've been plenty of stories about who must have done it and why. First suspect was us, of course, except that I didn't run away and hide. Then Arab terrorists, Israelis pretending to be Arab terrorists, Russian Mafia. There's been a huge security crackdown on all the international airports, and they doubled the personnel at the Mexican and Canadian borders. Meanwhile they tell the world they've been following a chain of evidence—"

"Straight to Jack Lawry," Cassie said.

"Right. They have their suspect now. A really good, really crazy suspect. He looks like us. He sounds like us. He was even with us for a while, and lots of people know it. The evidence they have is enough to convict him and his buddies in any court in the country. And he's got family in Quebec, so there's a link to the Canadian side too. Our guys look good, and so do the Canadians."

"But he didn't do it," Amber said.

"A technicality. When they take him to trial and he gets convicted, he'll be *officially* guilty. Nobody wants it any other way—except maybe Lawry. And don't go wasting any sympathy on him and his buddies. He's a psychopath, and they're vicious criminals, who deserve whatever they get."

"So that means we can go back to the farm, right?" Kenny said.

"Don't tell me you don't like Paradise!"

"It's boring! Especially with just *them.*"

"Well, nothing's going to be boring for long. I'm reactivating the farm. Sending some of the guys back there to keep it running, use it for training. It'll be official headquarters, the place where the Free Mountain Militia does its nonterrorist best to change the system. And to go on training a well-regulated militia to defend free American citizens in case their government ever decides to use force against them."

"So—when do we go back?" Kenny asked.

"You don't." Charles Landis turned to Mack. "You tell him, Mack. This is your baby."

"The farm is only a front. Paradise Park will be the real thing, operation central. Your dad will still be out there, talking and writing and pushing the politicians. But things are going to change from now on. The war's heating up."

"You kids and Cassie will be staying," Landis said. "Nobody knows about this place except the Cadre. They've been working on it for a long time now. We've already got most of the weapons stockpiled here, in a bunker under the trash heap, and a considerable number of facilities you haven't seen yet. Most of them are underground, connected by tunnels. Mack's here to stay now, and others will be coming. Mack will oversee the rest of the work."

"What about Elijah?" Amber asked.

"Ah, yes. That's the other news. It turns out Elijah Raymond wouldn't have been much of a bargaining chip even if we'd needed one. He has no living relatives. He's a ward of the state. They called off the search for him even before they quit looking for us. Missing and presumed dead, they say. Apparently nobody wants him back."

"Big surprise," Kenny said. "Then we don't need to keep him, right?"

"No."

"What are you going to do with him?" Amber asked.

"Take him back where we found him. Or someplace like it."

Cassie drained the last of her coffee and set the mug on the counter with a bang. "No," she said, her voice low but decisive.

Landis looked at her, his eyebrows raised. "No?"

"You can't do that," Cassie said.

"What would you suggest are the alternatives? Drop him off at some police station? Take him back to the mental hospital he escaped from?"

"He can't hurt us. He can't talk."

"We don't know that. We know he *doesn't*. Or he *hasn't*."

Mack, who had been leaning back in his chair, rocked

forward. "No way we can take that kind of chance."

"No way you can just leave him out in the woods either," Cassie said. "He wouldn't make it."

"I didn't think he would," Charles Landis said. "But he wouldn't have made it if we hadn't picked him up either."

"We can keep him."

"Oh, no way!" Kenny said.

"Keep an autistic child? Why would we do that?" Charles Landis asked.

Mack shook his head.

"Trust me on this one," Cassie said.

"I suppose you're going to tell me this has something to do with that bird," Landis said.

"There's more to it than that," Cassie said. She glanced at Amber, who looked down at her knee, the bruise almost completely gone, and nodded. "But yes," Cassie went on. "Partly it has to do with the bird. What do you know about shamans?"

"Medicine men?"

"They're called that too."

Mack snorted.

"This is some Indian thing, right?"

"I'm enough Mohawk to know there's things white people don't understand. Useful things." She turned to Landis. "You always say you value different perspectives."

"I do. But shamans? What does an African-American autistic kid have to do with shamans?"

"The boy's got something, something like the old shamans had. There's the raven, and there's more—more we've seen, probably more we haven't. It's all around him like a light. You made me a promise after Terrence died. You made it again when you married me. Are you going back on it now?"

Charles Landis sighed. "I said I'd always *listen* to you, not that I'd always do what you told me to do!"

"So listen. I'll take responsibility for the boy. He's with us for a reason. You know what some people call ravens? Wolf-birds." Cassie nodded at Landis's wolf tattoo. "Wolves and ravens hunt together. Ravens probably scout prey for the wolves, and wolves for sure provide food for the ravens. However it works, they go together, ravens and wolves."

"Reading the signs, eh? You sure you know how?"

"If it turns out I'm wrong, you can do whatever you have to do."

"Shamans!" Landis said. "Unbelievable."

The day Charles Landis was to come to Paradise Park, Elijah woke with the first hint of morning light. Nine years ago this day, August 25, 1991, just after dawn, he had been born into a family—a real family—in a world so distant from this place that it might have been in another galaxy. He had been born and wrapped in a blanket and named—Elijah for the Bible prophet, Germain for the father who had come and gone, and Raymond, his mother's last name. His had been a small family, only his mother and his great-grandmother. His world too had been small, the little gray weathered house with the tin roof, set like this one, among trees and mountains. He had been surrounded inside that house by love and outside by the creatures of the wild and by the infinite space of possibility.

Now, as the light grew around him, Elijah lay clutching his marble, filled with memories he'd thought were gone, along with the people and places they represented. Images tumbled into his mind—a teakettle pouring its steam into the air above a black woodstove, the smell of fresh corn bread, a cat stretched along the railing of a porch shaded by oaks and hickories, the sharp masked face of a raccoon looking down from the branch of a gnarled apple tree. And his mother, thin and light, a swirl of red dancing across a braided rug to a tune on the radio. He remembered the net of love that had supported him in that place even as his baby mind leaped into understanding at a rate that frightened Mama Effie, who saw and felt his difference from the first. It had been that difference that had lured their small family from the woods, from the mountains, to the city, where there might be more to feed his hungry mind.

The city had been a wrong choice, his mother had told him one night not long after they got there. But it was a choice they could not take back.

Mama Effie had told him there were no *wrong* choices, only choices that hurt some and had to be, *could be,* endured as long as necessary. But Mama Effie had died, and Elijah did not then and did not now believe her. There were plenty of wrong choices, and the people in his world had made them over and over, all of them the sort that could not be taken back.

Happy birthday. He let himself think the words to himself, and then he pulled his blanket up and turned over, rubbing his marble against his cheek. He was nine years old today, but the change made no difference. He promised himself he would think no more about this day or what it meant. It would be to him, as it was to his captors, just another day.

After breakfast Elijah watched Amber go out, taking water and a sandwich for lunch along with her notebook and binoculars to watch the loons on the lake and the great blue heron if it came. She headed around the lake toward the dam, but he did not follow her, as he often did, to watch with her. Kenny too went outside. Cassie had given them the day off from the work they'd been doing, chopping brambles away from the old greenhouse, but she had busied herself pulling stained and torn wallpaper off the walls in the cottage's living room. He went upstairs and closed himself into the space off Cassie's bedroom, where he slept. He made himself a nest of blankets on his cot and settled his thin, lumpy pillow behind his back. He had found a moldy copy of *Ivanhoe* in the stack of books Amber had rescued from the park lodge. It was a book he had started to read back at Laurel Mountain. He had not had time to finish it there. Here he had plenty of time.

But he did not read for long. This day was different for another reason, this one a reason he could not push away. It kept him from concentrating on the words and letting them conjure images in his head. The white-haired man with the tattoo was coming—the man whose effect on Elijah was not like anything he had ever felt before.

He thought of the man his mother had brought into their lives after Mama Effie died, the man who had beaten Elijah when he could not get away or hide in time, had beaten his mother and finally taken her from him. The growl Elijah had felt in his head whenever the man was working up to lashing out, the growl that so often warned him in time to escape, was something he had grown used to. That man had been all one thing, all brute force. Elijah had feared him, but he had understood him. And he had come to trust the growl of warning.

This man, Charles Landis, was different. Only the white hair said old man. He was tall and strong, with a voice that reached into Elijah in a way he found hard to resist, forceful, certain, and commanding. By look and sound the man drew Elijah, as he could tell everyone around the man was drawn. But his eyes, deep blue, were colder than winter. They sent a chill into Elijah's heart, touching something there that frightened him.

He pulled his marble out of his pocket and sat, spinning the marble in his open palm, allowing himself awareness only of color and movement. When Cassie called him to lunch, he put *Ivanhoe* beneath his pillow and went down. Through the whole meal, Kenny kicked him under the table. Elijah was used to it now. Almost

HIGH FRONTIER
SCHOOL LIBRARY

anywhere else Elijah could avoid the boy, feeling when he was getting ready to pounce in time to dodge a kick or punch or pinch. But at meals he was an easy target.

Afterward Elijah stayed in the kitchen when Kenny went upstairs to get into his swimsuit. Only after the boy had gone out did he go back and settle himself again to try once more to read. It was not long before he noticed the sensation, a shiver at the back of his neck. And he knew that Charles Landis was close. He dropped his book, leaped to his feet, and hurried through Cassie's room, down the stairs, and out the front door, letting it bang shut behind him. "Where are you going?" Cassie called as he ran down the porch steps. It was an automatic question, Elijah knew. Cassie understood she would not get an answer.

He did not wish to be there when Charles Landis arrived. He had no plan. He only wanted to get away. Maybe, he thought, he could stay away until the man had come and gone again.

Elijah slipped quickly into the thick woods behind the house. There was no footpath here, but little grew in the heavy shade of the close-set evergreens, so it was not difficult to make headway. The ground sloped slightly upward to his left, and he followed the line of the rise, moving steadily upward and away.

After a time the trees began to thin, the undergrowth spreading more thickly beneath them, and he found himself among large outcroppings of gray rock, splotched with gray-green and yellow lichens. He had gone far enough; the sensation at the back of his neck had gone. One particularly large rock seemed perfect for climbing, its sides pocked with depressions and crevices, its top fractured in a way that formed a sort of chair, its seat weathered smooth, its back upright among the branches of a pine that leaned against it. Elijah scrambled up and settled himself, turned away from Paradise Park, his back against the stone. He took a few long, deep breaths, letting his heart settle into a slow and steady beat.

The raven swooped low over his head and landed in a nearby tree. He was supposed to live, he knew. But what if Charles Landis came to stay? How could he stand to live here then?

Elijah didn't know how long he had been there when he became aware of a heavy scuffling in the thick coating of pine needles and leaf litter on the forest floor. He opened his eyes, turned toward the sound, and saw a black bear, its thick head moving from side to side as it made its way among the boulders. It was not more than ten feet away, had come up over the rise of hill to the right. And it was moving on a line that would take it directly beneath Elijah's boulder.

Suddenly it stopped moving and lifted its muzzle, its

nostrils quivering as it sniffed the air. Elijah held his breath. The bear sniffed again and then raised itself onto its back legs to stand at its full height, front paws crossed in front of its chest. Now it turned its head until it faced Elijah. Their eyes met. The bear made a whiffling, grunting sound. Elijah blinked and looked away, not wanting the bear to think he was challenging it. He focused instead on the bear's huge paws, the long, curving claws showing amidst the dark fur, and held himself as still as he could, taking shallow breaths.

Bears climbed trees, he knew. This one could surely climb this boulder. In fact, if it came only a few steps closer, it could swipe at his feet with one great paw and drag him down to the ground. But it did not come closer. It stayed exactly where it was, swaying slightly, snuffling quietly to itself. Then it did something astonishing. It settled itself on its haunches, looking for all the world like a dog sitting up and begging. Elijah looked up again, directly into its brown eyes.

As he did, as contact was made, eye to eye, Elijah felt a sense of swirling movement, of sinking, and then he found himself staring not at the bear but at himself, perched there on the boulder. It was as if he had been sucked out of himself and into the bear, as if his own mind was inside it now, behind its eyes. He felt its front legs hanging heavily from their shoulders, its paws resting lightly on its abdomen. Elijah blinked. Blinked again. The image before his eyes did not change. Red shirt, jeans, tattered sneakers, himself on the rock. Tree branches to either side, wreathing him in green needles. He felt the bear's breath, slow and heavy, moving in his nostrils, scented on the air a smell he had known all his life and yet not known at all, never consciously noticed—the warm scent of himself, of his own skin and hair and breath.

He was overwhelmed with sensation. The lingering taste of blackberries in his mouth. In the center of himself a deep, insistent hunger. The solid feel of the ground beneath him and the slight but noticeable movement of air on his face, his ears. The sound of a chickadee chirring overhead. The distant, hollow hammering of a woodpecker.

As suddenly as it had begun, the experience ended. Elijah was himself again, on the rock, looking into the soft brown eyes of the bear. The bear shook its head slightly, then pushed itself forward onto its front paws. It gathered its hind legs beneath it, lurched to its feet, and began moving again, shoving its way easily through the undergrowth. As it reached the base of Elijah's boulder, it slowed and rubbed its shoulder and back against the rock, as if scratching an itch it could reach no other way. Elijah had an impulse to lean down, stretch out one hand, and touch the bear's thick black fur. He did not. The heavy smell of the animal wafted up to him. It began moving again. It wound its way among the boulders, lumbering across the line of the hillside, and finally disappeared into the underbrush.

Elijah let out the breath he had been holding since the bear had rubbed against his rock. And found in his mind a thought he had not had before. There were times that were too dangerous to be part of. Too cold. Too dark. With nothing to eat, nothing to live on. It was not hard to know when those times were coming. The air changed, and the light. Those were the times of sleeping. Of hibernation.

Hibernation. It would be a slowing, stopping, almost like slipping into the glass world of his spinning marble. He reached into his pocket. His marble was not there. He reached into the other pocket. No. He patted the pockets against his legs, sure it had to be there, somewhere. Nothing. He launched himself off his rock, landing with such force that he fell forward onto his hands and knees. When and where had he had the marble last? He had had it all morning, spinning it on his hand. Then what? Then what? He had gone down for lunch. He must have left it on his cot. It must have gotten lost among the blankets.

Elijah started back toward the camp.

As he got closer to the house, he could feel the chill on his neck again. He did his best to ignore it. He needed to slip into the house, get to his room, get his marble. He couldn't remember ever being without it, not since Mama Effie had given it to him and he had discovered the way he could put himself into it, down into the silence of the center, where the blue and white swirl rested inside the clear glass. Long ago he had taught himself to sleep with the marble clutched in his fist, and he seldom woke with an empty hand. When the people at Laurel Mountain tried to take it from him, he had fought, he had kicked and bitten, and they had allowed him to keep it. How could he have left it?

When he reached the house, he hesitated at the front door. Charles Landis and the others were in the kitchen. If he was careful, he might get in, get to his room, and get back outside without being seen or heard.

"Mack's here to stay," he heard.

Elijah swallowed. Mack. It was Mack whose hands had dragged him from his place beneath the tree.

He picked his way carefully across the empty living room, its floor littered with the wallpaper Cassie had peeled from the walls, his sneakers making no sound on the faded linoleum. He eased his way up the stairs, stopping with every creak and groan of the old, dried wood. Still, the voices went on without interruption. At the top of the stairs he turned and hurried through Cassie's bedroom to his own space. His nest of blankets was as he had left it. The moldy book lay open on the cot, upside down.

Elijah moved the book, searched frantically among the blankets. The marble was not there. He knelt on the bare wood floor and peered into the darkness under the cot. Not there. He felt a catch in his throat. His marble had to be here somewhere. Carefully, methodically, he went through everything on the cot, shaking the pillow, lifting each blanket and shaking it. He felt along the edges of the canvas of the cot to see if there was a place the marble could have slipped into where he would not be able to see it. He took every bit of the clothing Cassie had given him out of the duffel bag that lay on the floor and felt into the corners when it was empty. It was no use. The marble was not there.

He stood in the middle of the small space and turned slowly all the way around, scanning every inch. He went into Cassie's room. It was not there either.

The chill on his neck was growing. Marble or no marble, he wanted to get away from here. He started down the stairs, less careful now to keep from being heard. What did it matter?

"Shamans," he heard Charles Landis's deep, smooth voice. "Unbelievable!"

Suddenly the man named Mack was at the door to the kitchen, looking up at him as he came down the stairs. "Speak of the devil," the man said. "I thought I heard something."

There was a scraping of chairs from the kitchen, and Charles Landis appeared behind the other man. In a few moments they had all come into the living room. The two men, Cassie, Amber, and Kenny all stood looking up at him.

"You're a lucky boy," Landis said. "Lucky to have a raven and luckier still to have Cassie."

Elijah heard what the man was saying, but he was looking at Kenny, whose face was set in a sneer, his light blue eyes cold and mocking. Slowly, deliberately, the boy reached into his pocket and brought out Elijah's marble. He held it up, being sure Elijah saw it. The adults turned away and went back into the kitchen. Amber followed them.

Kenny, grinning, stood facing Elijah, moving the marble back and forth, taunting. Then he turned and ran out the front door. Elijah ran down the stairs after him. By the time the screen door slammed behind

Elijah, Kenny was off the porch and heading for the lake. Elijah forced himself forward as fast as he could go, his legs pounding across the grass. He was gaining on the other boy, but only slightly. He would not get to him before he reached the edge of the lake. Elijah knew what Kenny was going to do.

Quork! The voice of the raven sounded above him, and a shadow passed over Elijah's head as the bird flew past. Kenny kept running, holding the marble above his head like a trophy.

Get it from him! Elijah thought toward the raven. He stopped running. There was nothing he could do now.

Kenny must have heard the sound of wings closing in because he turned in mid-stride and saw the huge black bird swooping toward him. "Screw you!" he yelled, and hurled the marble with all his might toward the water. Elijah watched as the marble Mama Effie had given him, the last vestige of his real life, arced up into the sun and then down, hitting the water and sending concentric rings of ripples across the surface of the still lake. The raven swept low over Kenny, so low the boy flung his arms over his head and ducked, but then flew on across the water, landing on the topmost branches of a pine on the other side.

Elijah and Kenny stood for a moment, staring at

each other. Kenny's sneer, Elijah saw, had slipped. *You are enemy,* Elijah thought. *I will remember that.*

But it seemed to him that Kenny was afraid. Just a little afraid.

part two

Dreamtime

WINTER

Pulling her sweater closer around her, Amber hurried into the chilly tunnel, heading for the storage barn. She hated being sent on errands and might have refused when the men ran out of staples and asked if she'd mind getting them a new box. But she'd gone to see how work was coming along on the interior of the War Room, so she couldn't very well claim she was too busy with her work in the computer center. The fact was, she needed a break from the job she'd been struggling with all morning—creating a game for the netsite's kid page based on the principles of sustainable agriculture. She wasn't sure it was possible. But if it was, it was probably Kenny who could do it, not her. He had a feel for what kids, especially the boys who visited their netsite, found exciting. Maybe he could make it a war game about bugs killing other bugs.

Suddenly the lights in the tunnel flickered and went out. Darkness shut down around her. Absolute darkness. She stopped, her breath caught in her throat, and stood still, her hands out in front of her as if to fend off some danger. She couldn't see her hands. She had to fight a momentary panic, as the darkness seemed to be a curtain of black surrounding her, smothering her. If she moved, it felt as if she would crash into a wall or step into one of those horrible pit traps Kenny had dug all over Paradise Park last summer.

There was nothing whatsoever to be afraid of, she told herself firmly. She was thirteen years old, not some little kid who got spooked by the dark. And this was just a tunnel she'd been in a million times. Behind her was the computer room, up ahead somewhere was the stairway, and at the top of the stairs were the storage barn and the daylight world of wind and snow. She felt for the ripply fiberglass panels that covered the tunnel walls. It wasn't the first time the power had gone out suddenly, just the first time she'd been alone in a tunnel when it happened. At least she hadn't lost something important on the computer! She took a few slow, deep breaths and began moving again, slowly but confidently, a hand on one wall to guide her.

She wasn't sure how near the stairs she had been when the lights went out, but she knew she'd be able to feel the place where the tunnel to the men's quarters branched off. The main tunnel led only to the stairs. There was no possible way to go wrong or get lost. It was just the intensity of the darkness that bothered her, so black she could almost *feel* it against her face.

Then she heard a sound behind her. Or did she? It could have been an echo of her own footsteps, the sound of her own breath coming back to her in the narrow space. She stopped and listened, her ears straining. There was nothing. Then, her hand on her chest as if to still the sound of her own heartbeat, she heard someone breathing.

No one had been in the tunnel before the lights went out, so someone, maybe someone on his way to check on the power, had come in after her. But if that was so, why didn't the person have a flashlight? He'd have known before he came in that it would be this kind of dark. "Who's there?" she asked, furious with herself to hear the tremor in her voice. How could she be afraid? Whoever was breathing in the darkness behind her, it was just one of the guys. Someone, she realized, playing a trick on her. Because otherwise he would have answered. "Kenny?" she said. "Whoever it is, go back and get a flashlight."

Footsteps, the sound of breath getting louder, closer, and then there were hands on her, one quickly finding her mouth, covering it so that she couldn't cry out. The hands were strong and hard, and she was shoved up against the wall. And then the hand that wasn't covering her mouth, wasn't pushing her into the rippled covering of the tunnel wall, began to move over her body. Amber curled her own hands into fists to pummel the body that closed in and pressed itself against her.

She struggled, kicking, hitting, until she managed to break free. Then she ran into the blind darkness until she tripped on the stairs, falling into them, cracking her knees and elbows as she went down. She scrambled up them, pushed open the door at the top, and was in the barn. Gray daylight, like the snow and wind, came in only through cracks around the sliding door in the loft, but it was enough to see by. She could make out the shapes of the objects around her, the snowmobiles and ATVs, the crates of building materials. She slammed the door, pulled and pushed a crate up against it, and then sat on the crate, getting her breath, listening to see if whoever the hands belonged to had followed her up. He had not.

She sat there for a long time, trying to decide what to do. She would not go back into the tunnel until the lights were back on. And even then how could she go back when she didn't know who the hands belonged to? If only she'd done something that would identify him, bitten him maybe, hard enough to draw blood. But she hadn't. It could have been any of them, or almost any. Not Stephen—or Jack—O'Donnell. She felt again the pressure of the body against her own, the size of the hands, the hot breath on her neck, and the lingering odor of sweat. The O'Donnell brothers were smaller, leaner. Duane or Virgil or Ham it could have been, though the thought that it might have been Ham, who traded jokes with her, teased her, prodded her always to be braver and tougher, made her sick to her stomach. It could even have been Mack, she supposed, though she couldn't quite believe that.

She ought to tell someone, Cassie at least, maybe her father. But telling would make it more real, make it something her father would have to deal with. Besides, what could she tell? She didn't know who it was. Even if she did know, it would be her word against his. And these were the men of the Cadre, her father's carefully selected inner circle, the men, as he'd told her often enough, he trusted with his life. How could she accuse one of them of—of what? She wasn't *hurt.* He hadn't done anything, really. She shuddered. Not *really.*

Elijah sat in the big chair near the living room wood-stove as the wind howled through the trees and around the corners of the cottage, blowing snow against windows and doors. His body, wrapped in a blanket, was curled into itself, arms around his legs, chin on his knees, rocking almost imperceptibly with the slow beat of his heart. But Elijah himself was elsewhere. Elijah was in the world he had come to call dreamtime.

He was a raccoon cub, moving stealthily through autumn midnight shadows along a muddy creek bank, stopping now and again to feel with long, sensitive fingers beneath stones in the rippling water for crayfish. Behind him and ahead he could hear the sounds of the other cubs, light splashes, the occasional *churr* of one checking for their mother's presence, and her soft answer. The moon reflected slivers of light from the moving surface of the water, making it difficult to see the darker presence of the stones, the flickering motion of minnows disturbed by his passing. An itch stopped him briefly, and he scratched industriously with his right hind leg before returning to his search.

The water was cold, the current a steady push as he felt along the gritty sand for the more solid shape of stone. *Sand, sand, stone, then a sudden swirl, the quick movement of scuttling crayfish darting away*. The cub that was Elijah snatched, closed his hand around the hard shell, and felt the crayfish struggling to free itself from his grip. He brought his catch up out of the water, moonlight glinting on the wet shell, the flailing legs and pincers. Gingerly, holding it with both hands at the edge of the water, he nipped with sharp teeth, both feeling and hearing the crunch of shell as he stilled its movement. Taste and texture flooded his mouth as he chewed, crunching shell, and swallowed, filling the hollow space of hunger in his middle.

Raising his head, Elijah heard a sound that did not belong, a metallic clicking, steady and monotonous. Something pulled at him, drawing him away from the dreamtime autumn night, back toward winter. He shook himself, trying to banish the clicking sound. He wanted to remain where he was, wanted to make his way back to the den, to spend the coming day in the warm presence of his mother and the other cubs.

Elijah lived in the world of Paradise Park when he had to, as the Cadre went about its work, refining and expanding the compound, but he participated in its life as little as possible. For a long time after the loss of his marble, he had felt like a rabbit chased from its hole and surrounded by enemies. Hibernation had been the bear's solution to a time of darkness and danger, but he couldn't find a way to make it work for him.

Without his marble he seemed to have lost not only its refuge but also the ability to reach his mind, as Taryn had taught him, into mountain or lake or tree. He had tried to build Tondishi, his imaginary land, as clearly in his mind as he had when he was little and had hidden under a bush, protecting himself with stories of the hero, Samson, who could fight off any enemy. But he could not lose himself there either. The old stories were too familiar, and new ones refused to come.

When Cassie discovered him reading, she had begun to give him books and printouts from the nets, creating a learning program for him, as she did for Amber and Kenny. But he finished reading what she brought him, too quickly to keep himself occupied even for the few hours a day she set aside for school. Besides, most of what Cassie brought him, the history of the American Indian since the coming of white men to the American continent, troubled him as much as the work of the Militia.

Then he had discovered dreamtime. As he often did, he had followed Amber that day in early October when she finished whatever job Cassie had given her to do and went out along the shore of the lake to look for the great blue heron and the loons that would soon migrate south for the winter.

The connection he felt with Amber gave him the only respite he had from the deep loneliness of this place and his fear of the men who, though focused for the moment on building their secret headquarters, had killed before and planned to kill again. Amber kept Kenny away from him whenever she could and always let Elijah walk with her if he wanted to. Sometimes when they sat sheltered by reeds or the bushes that overhung the lakeshore, she would talk.

Mostly she talked about her father and the work he was doing, preparing for the change that was coming, the change the Militia wanted to hurry along. She never mentioned killing. She talked about the damage humans and their civilization, their technologies, were doing to the earth, to the air and water. She talked about the destruction of the wilderness and the extinction of animal species. And how governments lied to people and took away their freedom. After the change people would be free again, she said, to learn how to live in harmony with the planet and one another.

Listening to her, he heard echoes of the conversations the Ark family had had back at Laurel Mountain. The four of them, Elijah, Doug, Miranda, and Taryn, had been taken from the main hospital to the log house they called the Ark to live together because of their minds. New minds, they were supposed to be. Mutations. They were not sick, like the others at Laurel Mountain; they were just different. Too different to fit in the regular world, the world Amber was describing, the world whose violence was clear in the news they encountered every time they sat at their computer screens and ventured onto the nets. And so they had talked about that world, about what they and the other new kids they had begun to find on the nets might be able to do about it. All of them had a sense of purpose, what Doug and Miranda had called a quest, something that drove the dream they were dreaming together. But the Ark kids had always been filled with doubt. Amber was not. Amber was certain, absolutely certain, that her father's work, the work she intended to do one day herself, would make a world that was better, one that would work.

On that bright autumn day, though, she had not been in a mood to talk. They had crossed the dam and settled themselves on the cement walk that led over the spillway. Her legs dangling over the water that ran smoothly over the rounded stone and cement hill of the spillway, Amber leaned against the lower railing and stared out across the still lake, the brilliant colors of the trees and the deep blue of the sky reflected in the water.

The loons were nowhere to be seen, and no heron stalked the shoreline, but after a time the raven swept down out of the sky and landed on a branch of a scarlet maple tree.

"Your bird," Amber said.

The raven muttered and shifted on the branch, but though the sounds it made sounded almost like speech, Elijah could understand nothing of them. For a long time the two of them—the three of them—remained still, the water running over the spillway the only sound, and then Elijah noticed a rustling in the leaves. A red squirrel bounded through the high grass along the dam, leaped up the trunk of a pine, and scampered up to the high branches above. Elijah watched the squirrel walk along a branch and then sit on its haunches, peering downward, looking directly into Elijah's eyes.

As had happened with the bear, Elijah felt a sudden swirling, sinking feeling and found himself looking down from above, at himself and Amber on the walkway. He could see the top of his own head, Amber's blond hair hiding her face, as she peered into the green water beneath her feet, where a school of minnows was rippling the smooth surface. He had a moment of dizziness at the feel of the narrow branch beneath his feet and then became aware of the balance provided by the tail that curled along his back. There was a strange sensation of quickening, speeding up, as if the blood were moving faster in his veins, his senses tuned to a different sort of time. His attention shifted. A little above his head a green pinecone jutted out from a twig. Without thought he stretched to it and, holding it between his paws, bit through its stem and sent it dropping to the ground beneath the tree.

The experience lasted longer that day than it had with the bear. Elijah stayed in the body of the squirrel as it hurried among the branches of the pine, biting off other cones, sending them falling to the ground, and then dashed headfirst down the trunk, gathered the cones at the base of the tree, and carried them into a hole beneath a stump farther along the dam.

Eventually Amber's voice had brought him back to himself, to the familiar feel and tempo of his own body, the thoughts of his own mind. "I'm going in," she said. "I'm getting cold."

Elijah nodded but did not get up. The squirrel disappeared into its hole as Amber headed back across the dam toward the cottage, and Elijah waited for it to appear again. When it did, though he'd hoped the experience would repeat itself, Elijah remained Elijah and squirrel remained squirrel.

In the next weeks it had happened again, with a mouse, a bat, a snake, until he found that he could make it happen whenever he wanted, not just with animals that were there in front of him but with any he could form an image of in his mind. It was like shifting himself out of his own body into the body of the other, becoming that other body the way he was a raven so often in his dreams. Except that for this he wasn't asleep.

It was not like making up the stories about Tondishi, which he did with his own mind. When he slipped behind the eyes of an animal, he took with him almost nothing familiar. He saw the world, then, as he had never seen or even imagined it, sensed as humans do not sense, experienced new feelings, *knew* in ways he had never known before. Sometimes it felt so real that he wondered afterward whether he might actually have *become* the animal, whether his own body might have vanished when he shifted, or whether his body, too, had shifted itself into this other form.

However it happened, dreamtime became his refuge. It was not like running away from Paradise Park; it was like entering a wholly different world.

Now, as a raccoon cub with the sharp taste of the crayfish on his tongue, Elijah saw another cub emerge from the deep shadow of the creek bank into the moonlight sheen on the water and cock its head as if listening. Could it hear the metallic clicking he was trying to ignore? Even as he wondered, Elijah saw the cub's image shimmer, its reality thinning as the world around it began to fade. Regretfully he let go of the bit of vanishing shell he could still feel between his hands.

Then the feel of the blanket around his shoulders, the click of metal on metal. He opened his eyes just enough to see through his lashes. The living room was empty, but Cassie was in the kitchen, whisking eggs in a metal bowl. He shivered as the door to the porch opened. Amber came inside, snow blowing in after her. She slammed the door behind her and stamped snow off her boots.

It was the sound of Cassie's whisk in the bowl that had come, somehow, into the dreamtime. But it wasn't only the sound that had pulled him back to winter. What had pulled him back was what he felt as Amber jammed her mittens into her pockets, took off her jacket, and hung it on a hook by the door. Her eyes were dark, troubled; her hands shook as she reached to unlace her boots. Elijah felt from her a storm of rage, confusion, fear more vivid than the wind that battered the door behind her.

Amber tugged her boots off and set them on the rubber mat beneath her jacket. Cassie called from the kitchen, "I'll have your omelette ready in a couple of minutes. Are you okay?"

Amber shook her head. She padded to the woodstove in her wool socks and held her trembling hands out to its warmth. She didn't want to talk about it now. Didn't even want to think about it. She glanced at Elijah, in his usual winter place in the chair by the stove, wrapped in his blanket. He seemed able to cut everything in the world off as if he lacked not only voice but mind. As if he had no thoughts, no feelings. *How does he do that?* she wondered. It was what she wanted to do now—cut off all thought, all feeling. But she couldn't.

Cassie came in and felt Amber's forehead. "You don't have a fever; do you feel sick?"

Again Amber shook her head. She pulled a chair close to the stove and sat down, her elbows on her knees, huddling close to the warmth. "I don't know what's the matter," she lied. "I just needed to get away. I didn't feel like eating in the lodge with the others."

"Maybe it's just the winter—cabin fever and a touch of claustrophobia. It happens to me sometimes, being underground day after day. The power outage probably triggered it. It gets so very, very dark down there."

Amber shivered and rubbed her arms, leaning even closer to the stove. It was not the cold she was feeling. *So very, very dark down there.* The memory flashed in her mind. *Hurrying down the dimly lit tunnel, the tiny pop as the lights blinked out, and the sudden, heart-stopping darkness.*

"At least we have daylight up here, even if it is freezing and blowing most of the time. That's why I like working in the greenhouse. We're all underground too much. It's a good idea to get back to the surface sometimes. Were you on the computer when the lights went off? Did you lose anything?"

Amber didn't answer at first. Again she saw the dim tunnel, the sudden darkness. She'd lost something, all right. But nothing so simple as a few paragraphs of writing or a net connection. "I'd been working on that game for the kid page when the guys doing the War Room ran out of staples. They asked if I'd go up and get a box, and I needed a break so—" She held her arms tightly across her chest, her nails digging into her upper arms through her sweater. "Never mind. I'll be okay."

Cassie shrugged and went back to the kitchen. As the

sound and smell of sizzling butter drifted in, Amber felt herself rocking ever so slightly forward and back, forward and back, as if she was hugging and rocking a child waking from a nightmare. She wasn't a child. And it wasn't a dream. It was real. Whoever had done this to her was someone she had known most of her life, someone she would go on seeing every single day. And he would go on seeing her. Whoever he was. One of her father's most trusted soldiers.

Soldiers. She'd wanted to be one herself. And all this time she had thought the only thing in her way was her age. How stupid she had been. *Too young* was a temporary thing. This wasn't. This wouldn't go away in time; it would get worse.

She hugged herself more tightly, her arms pressing the swellings on her chest as if she could crush them out of existence. What had happened was her own fault. Her body had betrayed her, would go on betraying her. Kenny had said it always—"a girl, only a girl." She knew now that she could never be a full member of the Cadre. Soldiers had to trust each other, depend on each other. How could she trust them—any of them—ever again? She was as smart as they were, smarter than most. But her mind didn't count in this. If that man in the darkness had wanted more of her, if she had not been able to break away, she could have done nothing to stop him.

She had found Cassie in the greenhouse as soon as the lights came back on, asked her to fix some lunch at the cottage. For just the two of them. She'd forgotten that Elijah might be here. She had wanted to talk to Cassie, ask her how she had learned to live as a woman in a world of men. They wouldn't have that conversation now, but it didn't really matter. She knew how Cassie had done it. She had married Charles Landis, the alpha wolf. That made her the alpha female, gave her real power, real authority over the men. For Amber it couldn't work that way.

"Look who's joined the living." Cassie's voice brought Amber back to the present. Cassie stood in the doorway, pointing at Elijah, who had dropped the blanket from around his shoulders and was sitting forward in his chair, his dark eyes fixed on Amber. "You don't have to go to the lodge for lunch. You can eat with us if you want," Cassie said to him. "It's ready."

Elijah didn't respond. He uncurled himself, put his feet down, and leaned toward Amber. She looked into dark eyes that were fixed unblinkingly on her own. After a moment she looked away. She had a feeling that he knew somehow about what had just happened to her. *That's silly,* she told herself. *He can't know. Cannot. There is no possible way.*

But she couldn't deny the feeling. He knew.

It had come to him like memory. *Hurrying down the dimly lit tunnel, the tiny pop as the lights blinked out, and the sudden, heart-stopping darkness.* It was as clear as the memories of Mama Effie, the Ark family, all the things that had happened to him, that he'd seen or heard or felt, that were stored somewhere inside, to be called up at will or stumbled over accidentally. But this thing had not happened to him. It was Amber's memory, flooding him with the feelings that radiated from her like the heat from the stove, the feelings that had called him back from the dreamtime. Now they washed through him as he remembered the darkness, the body, the hands.

Elijah ate the omelette Cassie served him, barely aware of the sounds around him, the clinking of forks on plates, a voice asking for salt, another responding. He felt himself pushed one way, then another by fear, confusion, fury that had, without his willing it, without his permission, become his own. Fury. It shoved at him like the wind driving snow against the walls of the cottage, demanding that he do something. But what? He chewed and swallowed, chewed and swallowed, listening to the sounds in his head.

When he had finished eating, he went back to his chair, wrapped himself again in his blanket. Cassie was talking now, telling Amber to stay at the cottage the rest of the day, take a nap, read a book, take a break. She would come check on her later.

Elijah looked up as Cassie, bundled now against the weather, opened the front door and hurried out, leaving a swirl of snow that blew onto the linoleum floor and melted there. Had he imagined the voice of the raven swirling in with the snow? He shivered and drew the blanket more tightly around his shoulders. Amber was moving in the kitchen now, stacking dishes on the counter, clattering silverware into a dishpan.

Perhaps there was something he could do after all, something he could find out, at least, in dreamtime. He took a slow, deep breath, listening into the wind for the raven to repeat its call. He had never used the dreamtime the way he wished to use it now. But he had never tried.

Raven, he thought, and imagined himself outside, perched on a tree branch, eyes slitted against the driving snow. Suddenly he felt the familiar sinking sensation, and then the snow was there against his eyes as his claws gripped the tree branch. He had not, this time, lost the self he knew himself to be. He was at once both fully raven and fully Elijah. He blinked, shifted his weight from one foot to the other, and then launched himself off the tree branch, flying out into the sky above the cottage, the snow beating hard against his wings. He angled them and, slipping sideways against the current of the wind, flew out across the frozen lake and over the buildings of Paradise Park. He flew lower, out of the worst of the wind, and skimmed over the old trash dump, its piles of rusted engines, broken and rotted boat hulls, shattered furniture, nothing now but humps in the white expanse. Snow hid the trash dump now, as the dump hid the bunker of guns and explosives beneath it. He swooped past two crumbled cabins, broken walls jutting up through the drifts, and landed on the roof of the two-story lodge. A huge piece of the old roof's center had crumbled and fallen in. What could not be seen from above was the other roof, the new one that had been built beneath the ruin, covering the renovated first-floor main gathering room. A thin plume of smoke rose from the old stone chimney, barely visible in the swirl of windblown snow.

Elijah dropped onto the porch, landed on the railing, and peered in through the front window. The men had gathered for lunch. Ham LaFontaine stood at the end of one of the long wooden tables, pulling a heavy sweater over his head. Stephen O'Donnell, the Cadre's cook, turned hamburgers in a huge skillet on the stove, while his brother, Jack, got ketchup and mustard out of the refrigerator. Mack Sturdivant, scratching a week's growth of beard, sat at a table next to the tall silver coffee-maker, sipping gingerly at a steaming mug of coffee. At the other end of the table Duane Bruder was trying to lay out a game of solitaire as Kenny snatched cards and turned them over almost as fast as he could lay them down. Virgil Conway, the flat-faced blond who had wanted to leave Elijah behind the day he had been taken, came in from the hallway wearing a parka, which he took off and threw over the back of a chair.

Elijah could see that Mack was saying something to Virgil, gesturing at him with his coffee mug, but he couldn't make out the words.

Virgil frowned, his face reddening as he answered. Mack spoke again, and Virgil went to find a place at another table.

For a long time Elijah stayed where he was, trying to reach his mind into the minds of the men inside, to get behind their eyes. He focused on one after another. But it was like beating himself against the window glass. He was as separate from them as the raven none of them noticed on the porch railing outside. Maybe the dream-time worked only with animals, with minds less complicated than the minds of humans. Or maybe there was something about this kind of reaching he didn't know. For a moment he felt a fierce longing to be back at the Ark, to hear Taryn's voice explaining about reaching, Miranda and Doug complaining that they couldn't do it. He shook himself free of the memory, surprised when his movement raised a pair of black wings on a porch railing in the wind. Elijah or raven, he had nothing to offer Amber. He could not use the dreamtime as he had hoped to use it.

The low call of a raven's voice seemed to pull Elijah up into the wind and snow above the lodge. Moments later he was back in the cottage, the heat of the woodstove warming his face. He sat for a moment, adjusting to the weight of his body around him.

Amber was sitting in a chair on the other side of the woodstove, a book open in her lap. She held a mug of hot chocolate in both hands, breathing its steam, staring off into space. He could feel her confusion, her fury. But now there seemed to be very little fear.

"I'm sorry," Elijah said aloud. So long unused, his voice caught in his throat. The sound that came out was a kind of croak, more like the raven's voice than the words he'd meant to say. Amber looked at him. Elijah cleared his throat and tried again. "I'm sorry." He had been silent so long he barely recognized his own voice.

Amber's eyes grew round with surprise. "You can talk!"

Elijah nodded. "I'm sorry," he repeated. "I wanted to find out who it was—I tried—"

"Who it was?"

"In the tunnel. I couldn't."

Amber just looked at him for a moment, her mug of hot chocolate poised between them. "How do you know about the tunnel?"

He had no clear answer for her question. But it was as if those first words had broken a dam that had been holding back a torrent of speech that he couldn't stop. He told her about the connection he had felt with her from the first night when the image of the baby rabbits had filled his mind. He told her what had happened in the tunnel, everything he had remembered even though it had happened to her, not to him. And then he told her about reaching, about the Ark family and how Taryn had taught them to do it. He told her about being mutations, new kids with new minds, and the other kids around the world who were like them. He told her about dreaming together and the quest that they didn't understand. When at last the torrent dwindled to an end, Amber was sitting on the floor next to his chair, her arms clasped around her knees. She shook her head.

"There's no way any of this makes sense. But the memory you have of the tunnel is exactly how it was. Exactly." She shook her head again, her face bewildered. "I never told anyone, not anyone, about those baby rabbits."

Elijah was shivering. He pulled the blanket tighter, but it didn't help. "I couldn't tell who it was in the tunnel." He couldn't remember everything he'd told her when the words began to come, but he didn't think he had told her about the dreamtime, about becoming animals. "I tried to find out, but I couldn't connect with any of the men."

"How did you do it with me?"

"I didn't. It just happened."

"We need to tell Cassie," Amber said. "She's said all along you've got something. You're like the old Indian shamans, she says. The way you healed my knee that time, the way the raven follows you. But she needs to know about this other, this . . . connecting . . . thing. Reaching."

Elijah shook his head. He had talked to Amber because he couldn't help himself, but he was not ready to talk to anyone else. "No. If you tell her, I won't talk again."

"But—"

"No." Elijah shook his head and went on shaking it, his mouth set in a hard, tight line, until Amber shrugged.

"Okay. Okay."

"What will you do about the man in the tunnel?" he asked her then. "About not knowing?"

Amber smiled grimly. She reached into her pants pocket and pulled out a thick silver and red knife marked with a silver cross in a circle. Elijah could see that it had many blades, folded into the slots along each side.

"Cassie's Swiss Army knife. I found it in the drawer in the kitchen. She says it's too heavy to carry all the time." Amber put the knife back in her pocket. "I don't care."

Elijah nodded. The knife did not seem to him a good weapon. But she was not afraid anymore. For that a knife in her pocket seemed to be enough.

The huge bird came like a black shadow, plummeting toward him out of the sky, so wide it blocked the sun and turned the world dark around him. As it came closer, Kenny saw the red eyes, the sharp, heavy beak and flung his arms over his head to protect himself. It swooped over him so close that he could feel the wind of its passing against his scalp. As it climbed into the sky and wheeled around for another pass, Kenny struggled through the heavy mud that dragged on his feet, reaching desperately for the hunting rifle that seemed to float in the air in front of him just out of his reach. He was crying now, sobbing with frustration and terror.

The bird came swooping again, its beak open, so huge it looked as if it could swallow him, screaming, screaming as it came.

Kenny woke up, the echo of the bird's scream ringing in his ears, and felt the rawness in his throat that told him the scream had been his own. He blinked and assured himself that he was awake, that the bird had been nothing more than a dream. It was gone now, the darkness around him not the shadow of a monster but an ordinary winter night.

"Kenny? You okay?"

Cassie's voice from across the hall brought him fully awake. As he started to answer her, he recognized the old familiar dampness beneath him, the growing chill. His stomach clenched. He had promised himself that this would never happen again. He was eleven years old now. A soldier. It couldn't be!

It hadn't happened for months, and he had been so sure it was over. The last time had been in the summer, and he had managed to keep it a secret. It had been only his underpants and a sheet he needed to deal with then, and he'd sneaked them out to the canoe when he went fishing, rinsed them, and spread them in the woods to dry.

He reached down to find out how bad it was and groaned. Not just pajamas, but sleeping bag too. Everything wet through. Unless he could hang the sleeping bag by the woodstove downstairs, it might not dry out in a whole day. How could he keep it secret this time?

"Kenny?" Cassie's voice came again.

"A nightmare," he called, trying to make his voice sound groggy. Maybe, if she didn't think he was fully awake, she wouldn't bother him.

But then he heard her footsteps. An instant later his door opened, and she came in, her flashlight making a pale gold circle on the floor. "Go away," he said. "I don't need you."

"Was it your old dream again?" she asked.

"No. Go away!" Kenny turned his back on her, willing her to retreat. She didn't. The beam of her flashlight fell on the wall now, as she came closer. She touched his shoulder, and he jerked away from her hand. "Leave me alone!"

Then she sat on the edge of the bed. For only a moment. When she stood again, Kenny knew that she knew. He was furious at her, wanted to hit, to kick, to stop her from saying anything, stop her even from knowing. He had told her not to come in, to leave him alone. Why couldn't she listen? Why didn't she ever, ever listen to him? For a moment there was no sound except his breathing, and then Cassie was moving, opening his dresser drawer. She didn't speak. She only tossed him a pair of pajamas and then went out, leaving the door open behind her. Kenny stayed where he was, sick with shame and disgust, and then she was back. He felt a weight against his feet.

"Blankets. Fold your sleeping bag and put it in the corner." Her voice was low, but there was an edge to it. "We'll deal with it later."

Then she was gone. As his door closed behind her, he heard her voice again. "Go back to bed, Elijah. It's nothing."

Kenny held very still, listening. But there were no more sounds. What was the difference in her voice whenever she spoke to Elijah? A kind of softening. The way her eyes seemed to change when she looked at him, the way she touched him when she passed nearby—a finger brushing his arm, a quick touch on the head or the back. As if he was something special. Well, he wasn't. Sick maybe, brain-damaged, but nothing special.

When he was sure Cassie and Elijah had gone back to bed, Kenny threw off his sleeping bag and stepped out onto the cold wooden floor. Shivering so that he could barely manage the buttons, he changed into the other pajamas and shoved the wet ones into the sleeping bag. He threw the whole sodden bundle on the floor in the corner, wrapped himself in the blankets Cassie had brought, and got back into bed. For a long time he lay there, the blankets rough against his skin, unable to get warm, to stop shivering.

This thing wouldn't go on happening, he told himself. Grown men didn't have this problem. Only boys. Eventually they outgrew it. Every one of them. It didn't happen to soldiers in the barracks or out in the field. And it wouldn't happen to him anymore either. *This was the last time. Absolutely the last time.*

Then it occurred to him that if Cassie had spoken to

Elijah, the boy must have been up, out of the little room off Cassie's where he slept. Had he heard or seen anything? Had he seen Cassie with the blankets and guessed what was going on? Brain-damaged the kid was supposed to be, but Cassie gave Elijah work to do, books to read, just as she did for him and Amber. Kenny refused to think about it. Elijah didn't know anything about this; that was all there was to it. He didn't, couldn't know.

He closed his eyes, and instantly the memory of his nightmare came back to him, the black bird swooping down out of the sky. He opened his eyes and stared into the darkness, so much deeper, even with the snow softening it, than in the city, where there were streetlights, car lights. It was quieter in the woods than in the city too. The only sound he could hear was the wind around the edges of the cottage, moving the trees so that now and again there was a low thump as snow was shaken off the trees onto the ground below.

Kenny didn't want to sleep again, to dream, didn't want to find his feet stuck in mud or tar, or glued to the ground, his weapon forever unreachable and that bird, crazily bigger than any bird who'd ever lived, coming to get him. It wasn't the first time he'd had the dream. It had come to him at least twice before that he could remember, the first time the night after he'd thrown

Elijah's stupid marble in the lake. Each time it came, the dream seemed to be worse than before, the bird bigger, the difficulties greater. Dreams cheated. In real life he would never be so helpless. In real life he would have a weapon, and the bird would be only a bird.

MARCH

A cold rain pattered against the glass of the rebuilt greenhouse as Amber worked, planting seeds in peat pots and filling flats that would be kept in the dark under the worktable until they sprouted and had to be brought out into the light to grow. There was still snow on the ground outside, melting at the edges with the rain, but it all would turn to ice in the night. "Forcing spring" Cassie had called the work she was doing, so that there would be enough time for harvest in the short Adirondack growing season.

The idea was to make Paradise Park as self-sustaining as possible, and the garden was Cassie and Amber's job. Back in November Ham and the O'Donnell brothers had found where the original vegetable garden had been and cut a few trees that had grown high enough to shade it. As soon as the ground was workable outside, they would till it so the greenhouse plants could be set out and the short-season hybrid seeds could be planted. There would be lots of work to do between now and the end of the summer, when they'd see how their first harvest went, but Amber felt good about the start she was making. It felt as if today she was making her first concrete contribution to their future.

As she poured water onto the newly seeded pots, the word that had been in Amber's head when she woke up that morning was still going around and around like a stuck song. *Tondishi, tondishi, tondishi.* Amber thought it must have come from something she'd read, some homeschool assignment, though she couldn't remember what it might have been, so she asked about it when Cassie was showing her what to do with the seeds.

"It wasn't in anything I've had you read," Cassie told her. "Maybe you saw it on the nets somewhere, and it just got stuck in your head.

But that wasn't it, Amber knew. Because the word was more familiar than that. It seemed to bring with it images, feelings, too clear to be dismissed, too vague to be brought into focus, like a dream that's there when you wake up but fades before you can get a solid hold on it. Except this felt deeper than a dream, more like a memory of something real in her life. She'd be glad when Elijah came to help her with the planting. Maybe talking to him would get the word unstuck and let it fade away.

Cassie had told her she'd send him over to help as soon as he finished the book he was reading. It had been nearly three months since Elijah had first spoken to Amber, and still Cassie didn't know he could talk. When anyone besides Amber was around, the boy was as silent as ever, only his eyes showing that he was there, watching and understanding what went on around him. As sharp as Cassie was about other things, Amber thought, as she bent to set a flat of tomato seeds on a shelf under the table, she didn't catch on about Elijah, still thought that however fast he read any book she gave him, and whatever weirdness there was about him and his raven or his ability to heal with his hands, he had some kind of brain damage that kept him mute. Cassie thought the people at the hospital had been right about him.

Amber knew better. It wasn't that Elijah talked a lot. Even with her he tended toward silence, nodding or using gestures sometimes as if he had forgotten that he could speak perfectly well. But when he did talk, it was clear that he was as sharp as anybody Amber had ever met. No way he could be that smart and brain-damaged too. He knew things probably nobody else his age in the whole world knew. He'd read books Amber had only heard about. And once when she'd been struggling with a math problem, he had leaned over her shoulder and solved it for her. Afterward he explained how he'd done it, and his explanation was clearer than the explanation her on-line tutor had provided.

He hardly talked at all about his time in the hospital, but he'd learned to use computers there and had gone out on the nets, which was probably how he knew about so many of the things Amber told him were going wrong in the world, especially the ones that had to do with war or terrorism or violence of any kind. But he didn't react to that stuff the way Kenny did, with the kind of excitement the men felt about football or basketball. When Elijah talked about those things, he would tense up as if it was all he could do not to run back to the cottage and hide out in his old rocking trance.

Amber had tried one day to get him to understand what her father had explained to her so often—that sometimes violence was necessary. Good even. That you couldn't change the world, even for the better, without violence. Because the world was full of people doing bad things who wouldn't just stop because somebody told them to stop. She'd reminded him that if the American Indians Cassie had him reading about hadn't fought back against the white men invading their territory, they might have been wiped off the face of the earth instead of driven onto reservations that, bad as they were, at least allowed them to survive. "If Indians hadn't taken some scalps, Cassie wouldn't be here." Elijah had said nobody could know what might have happened if the Indians had found some other way to resist besides killing people.

She'd asked what other way, and he said he didn't know. Except that the Ark kids he talked about, the ones with the minds that could do new things, thought they might be able to use their minds, linked together, to tame the violence in others. Imagining its happening the way a wild animal could be tamed. He didn't really know if they could have, though. The time they tried, one of them didn't do what he was supposed to. Now they weren't together anymore, so there wasn't any way to test it. Amber told him the whole idea sounded like pure fantasy. Violence was real, so people had to fight back for real. Before he'd had a chance to say anything more, Kenny had appeared, and Elijah went back to playing mute. They hadn't talked about it since.

What she didn't get was how Elijah could know so much about the violence that was going on in the world and not see that refusing to fight back only—always—made things worse. Weakness brought out the worst in the people who would do others harm. It was why she still carried the knife with her every single day, even though no one had tried anything again. She made sure she was never alone with any of the men, not even the ones she was sure hadn't done it. But always she had the knife, just in case.

Elijah needed to know the danger of seeming weak with Kenny. He never, never fought back when Kenny tormented him. If he could get out of his way, he did. If he couldn't, he accepted whatever Kenny did as if nothing had happened. Far from stopping Kenny, it only pushed him to look for something worse to do next time. Even the time Kenny piled snow against the door of the cottage's latrine when Elijah was inside and he was stuck in there half a day and practically froze to death, Elijah hadn't taken any kind of revenge.

When she told him that refusing to fight Kenny only made him worse, Elijah shook his head and said that *Kenny* made Kenny worse. He didn't get it that it didn't matter how you said it, or whose fault it was, Kenny would keep trying to hurt him unless he fought back hard enough to stop him.

Now the greenhouse door opened from the outside, and Elijah came in, brushing rain off his hair as he closed the door.

"Why didn't you come through the tunnel?" Amber asked as he took off the winter jacket he was wearing and hung it, dripping, from a hook that held a coiled garden hose.

"I like it outside."

"Well, me too. But not in this weather."

"Any weather."

Amber shook her head. There were times she thought maybe there had been a reason for Elijah to be in a mental hospital after all. "I'm just glad you're here. I need somebody to talk to so I can get this stupid word out of my head."

"What word?"

"Tondishi. It was there when I woke up this morning, and I can't get rid of it."

Elijah stood very still, looking at Amber, his eyebrows knitted in a quizzical frown. "Tondishi?"

Amber nodded. "You've heard of it?"

"It's the name of a country I used to tell myself stories about. I made it up."

While he helped Amber with the planting, Elijah told her his Tondishi stories. In every one of them the hero, Samson, defeated all his enemies. As he talked, the feelings and images that had clung to the word in Amber's mind cleared and fitted into the stories, as if she'd heard them before, though she was certain she never had. And behind Elijah's voice she felt something else that she couldn't quite bring into focus, some fearful, dark thing.

When he finished telling her all he could remember, she told him what had come to her so strongly as she listened, that Samson was very like her father, willing to fight if he had to, to stop the evil in the world.

"See? It's what I've been telling you all along, and it's right there in your own stories. Fighting isn't wrong if you do it for the right reasons. In the battle between good and evil, good *has* to fight or evil wins."

Elijah frowned and set a row of pots into an empty flat, one at a time, as carefully as if they were made of something terribly fragile. He didn't answer.

"But I still don't understand, if you made Tondishi up, how I could have known about it? It's like I've heard the stories before. Are you sure you aren't just remembering stories somebody told you when you were so little you don't remember the telling part?"

Elijah shook his head. "I wasn't ever that little." He looked at her for a moment, frowning. "I wasn't sure before, but I thought so."

"Thought what?"

"The connection doesn't just go from you to me; it goes from me to you. If you dreamed Tondishi, it means you dreamed my memory. That's something Ark kids can do. It means you're one too."

Amber looked out through the condensation on the greenhouse windows, so heavy she couldn't even make out the dark shapes of the trees at the edge of the forest. It had stopped raining. "I don't understand. What does that mean?"

Elijah hadn't answered Amber's question. He didn't know the answer.

That night, when he had settled under his blankets in the little room off Cassie's, he focused down inside himself in a way he hadn't dared to do since he ran away from Laurel Mountain. He was trying to find the living sense of the Ark family. He searched first for Doug, filling his mind with the image of him that was strongest and deepest: Doug in cut-off jeans and a faded T-shirt, sitting on the porch of the log house they called the Ark, playing his flute, the liquid notes wafting through the trees, weaving the web that had first pulled Elijah in, that afterward seemed to hold them all together. But the image was all he found, as dry and empty as a chrysalis when the butterfly has flown.

He tried Miranda, visualizing her at the keyboard of one of the Ark computers, tapping out a message in some language only she and the person she was writing to on the other side of the world understood. But Miranda too was gone.

Last of all he tried Taryn, whose loss had meant the

end of the Ark family, had sent him out to the mountain intending to die, out where the Militia had found him. He visualized Taryn, black hair falling forward over her face, kneeling in the moss at the foot of a tree, looking intently at a pale purple wildflower as she reached her mind into it, communing with it.

And felt something. A tiny sense of something, a thread as fine as spider's silk. He held his breath, concentrating on the sense of that thread and the image of Taryn with the flower. Little by little the thread grew until he felt it warming into certainty. Taryn was out there somewhere, no longer sealed off by the drugs she'd been given when she was snatched from the Ark. He could get no more than that, no images, no sense of where she was, what she was doing. It was enough. Doug had thought the drugs might break the link completely, destroy whatever it was in Taryn's mind that let her connect. But that hadn't happened. However fine and fragile it was, if this one thread existed still, there was hope for more, hope that one day the web that had held the four of them together, that had reached across the nets and into the broader world to the others, might be woven again.

Elijah pulled his blankets more tightly under his chin. He didn't know what it meant that Amber, daughter of the Wolf, was one of them, didn't know how she might fit into their web. But for now he could do nothing but trust whatever force was at work, whatever force had brought Taryn back to life in the deepest part of himself.

A U G U S T

It was August again, a muggy, overcast day, a little more than a week before Elijah's tenth birthday, and Charles Landis was at Paradise Park. He had been there for days, longer than he had ever stayed before, charging the air with tension and sending the men into a frenzy of activity. Life at the cottage had changed from the moment he arrived, moving into the room with Cassie and turning Elijah out of his space, as Landis always did when he came, to sleep under the eaves in a corner of the attic outside Amber's room. The family ate in the lodge with the men at lunch, but breakfasts and dinners, to which Mack was usually invited, were eaten at the kitchen table in the cottage, Amber and Cassie doing the cooking and cleaning up as Landis sat and talked about the political work he'd been doing, the allies and enemies who helped or hindered his efforts. Sometimes he talked long into the night about his dreams for the new world that was to come from the Militia's work.

Amber, beside herself with the fact of her father's presence, had doubled her efforts, as had all the others, working with such intensity that she took no notice of Elijah or anything else. Though she often stayed up late to listen to her father's monologues, she got up early and began her work before breakfast. She cultivated the garden, harvested corn and beans, cucumbers and tomatoes, peas and carrots, spent hours in the lodge kitchen, helping Stephen O'Donnell with canning, and in between, when she could get his attention, showing off for her father what she had learned in Cassie's homeschool project on wilderness survival. Kenny, on the other hand, followed the man like a puppy until he would be sent off to do some chore that would get him briefly out from underfoot.

As he had almost every day since Landis came, Elijah, followed by the raven whose companionship he had long come to depend on, headed for his boulder to get away, to launch himself into dreamtime. As usual, no one bothered him; not even Cassie or Amber seemed to notice his absence.

As he climbed the hill, he saw that mushrooms were beginning to sprout among the moss. Mushrooms were not among the wild foods Cassie let any of them gather. "Too dangerous," she decreed. "Too many poisonous look-alikes." When Cassie set Amber and Kenny their summer task of learning wilderness survival, she had told them that their lives might very well depend one day on what they could learn and started them researching information on the nets. For the most part, what they read about there they were then supposed to practice in real life. All summer they had experimented with the eating of wild plants.

Elijah looked across the hillside at the dark, moss-covered stump of a tree that had fallen so long ago that its trunk and branches had crumbled entirely away, absorbed into the forest floor's cycle of life, and grinned to himself. Both Amber and Kenny knew that fallen trees, the logs and stumps that studded the ground beneath the growing timber, could be an important source of food. In the rotten wood lived grubs and termites and the larvae of other insects that were like small packages of protein, available at any time of year to any creature that could dig them out. But to them that was just information. Only Elijah, living during dreamtime in the bodies of the animals that made the wilderness their home, had actually eaten such food.

Elijah wondered if there would really come a time when the lives of the Cadre would depend on surviving without the supplies that came now by truck over old logging roads and by ATV or snowmobile, on ever-changing trails so that the outside world wouldn't suspect the secret life of Paradise Park. If so, could they possibly raise enough, hunt enough to get along? He pictured Kenny biting into a white squirming grub. It was just possible that if it came to eating grubs, Kenny would rather starve to death.

Even the thought of Kenny seemed to bring into Elijah's mind the buzz that had begun to warn him of Kenny's presence before the boy could carry out a plan to trip or kick or punch. If Amber was right that Elijah's refusal to fight back was making Kenny ever meaner, more determined in his assaults, at least the boy's growing menace had reached a level that provided an alarm.

In the distance thunder rumbled. Elijah reached his boulder and climbed up onto it. The air felt heavy, still, the leaves unmoving on the birch tree beyond his boulder. Probably he would not be able to stay long. Rain was almost certainly on its way. From behind he heard the sound of the raven's wings, and the great bird swooped low over his head to land in the birch.

Kenny had gone to the War Room that morning to catch Charles Landis after his strategy meeting with Mack. He had finally worked up the nerve to try to convince his father to let him be part of the current operation. He was more than halfway to his twelfth birthday. There were full soldiers his age in some countries, soldiers who had their own AK-47s, who used grenades and even rocket launchers. He'd read about them.

For two days he'd been planning his argument, and Ham had promised to back him up. During the paint ball war games at the farm last month, Kenny had single-handedly taken out half of Ham's troop by rigging a snare that dropped out of the trees as they went under it and then sniping at them from the topmost branches of a tree. He'd managed to turn what he'd learned about hunting animals in Cassie's stupid survival project into a strategy for war. Even Mack had praised his ingenuity.

There was an operation coming up, Kenny knew. The level of activity, the nighttime coming and going between Paradise Park and the farm, had increased. Maybe this operation would be as big as the Northway bombing. But even if it wasn't, no matter what it was,

Kenny wanted to be in on it. He was tired of being treated like a child.

When he found them in the War Room, his father and Mack, coffee mugs at their elbows, had been bent over a map marked with red circles. As soon as Kenny put his head in the door, before he had a chance so much as to open his mouth, his father had waved him away as abruptly, as harshly as if Kenny was some kind of bothersome insect. He hadn't even spoken, just flapped his hand at him in total dismissal.

Face burning, Kenny had shut the door and headed down the main tunnel, past a couple of regular Militia men who had come in the night before, trying to look as if he had intended to come this way all along. It was the tunnel that led to the storage barn. Kenny climbed the stairs and closed the door behind him. No one was there. Most of the men would still be in the lodge, dawdling over breakfast with neither Mack nor Landis to send them on their way.

He stood in the dim interior of the shed, fuming, furious, wanting to hit something, kick something. It had never occurred to him when he planned his argument that his father wouldn't even hear it! That he'd wave him away as if nothing he could possibly say could be worth the time it took to say it. Kenny had expected him not only to listen but to agree, to set him to work on something having to do with the operation immediately. What could he do now? It was early. If he went back to the cottage, Cassie might see him and give him something stupid to do, some lesson or some chore that would have nothing to do with the Militia's real work.

He paced among the ATVs, kicking at their tires, his stomach churning. He would go hunting, he decided finally. No one was allowed to fire a weapon at Paradise Park except in the underground firing range, but Kenny didn't hunt with a gun. He had been practicing all summer with the bow and arrows he'd made for himself. He'd managed to get a red squirrel the week before, his first kill. He hadn't told anyone. Cassie, with that Indian thing she had about the unity of all living things, insisted that killing animals was only for survival, when you needed them for food. It didn't occur to her that if you were going to be able to hunt your own food, you had to practice. It wasn't like going to the grocery store and picking up a package of hamburger, something you could do the first time you tried.

Kenny had skinned the squirrel and buried its carcass. He'd cleaned the skin as well as he could and put it in a box under his bed. Someday he planned to make himself something—a hat maybe—from the skins of the animals he shot. He wouldn't be able to take down anything big, not unless he could get himself real arrows with steel tips and a bigger, stronger bow. But it gave him a sense of pride to know that the weapon he'd made for himself was capable of killing, even if it was only something as small as a squirrel. And even greater pride to know that he could do it. Squirrels were so fast some people might have trouble getting one with a gun, much less a homemade arrow.

He went out into the muggy gray morning and hurried around the lake to get his bow and the quiver full of arrows he'd made from the toolshed in back of the cottage. He was about to start back when he saw Elijah come around the cottage and head into the woods behind it. There was no trail, but he was moving quickly and purposefully, as if he knew where he was going. It didn't occur to Kenny to follow until the raven flew down out of the sky and into the woods, winging its way between the trees after Elijah.

Kenny tightened his grip on his bow. The raven would make a perfect target, he thought. If he could get a squirrel, he could get a raven. Besides, Kenny thought grimly, it was high time somebody killed that stupid bird. Show them all once and for all that there was nothing magic about it. Nothing magic about Elijah either. Just an oversize crow and a crazy little black kid. The Cadre would be better off without both of them. There was nothing he could do about Elijah, but he could kill the bird.

Kenny had started after them then, pleased to see that he could follow the trail Elijah was leaving as he moved so carelessly through the woods, scuffing leaves out of the way, kicking loose bits of moss, breaking twigs. He didn't need to stay close enough to see Elijah or even hear him.

As the raven swooped over his head, its wings almost brushing Elijah's hair, there was another sound, so slight Elijah barely heard it. A hiss. A tremor in the air, and then, suddenly, the impact of something hard, sharp, striking his upper arm so powerfully it nearly jolted him off the boulder. There was a hot stab of pain, and Elijah turned to see the arrow that had pierced his arm, point jutting out on one side, feathers quivering on the other.

Elijah stared at the arrow in an oddly disconnected way, as if it had nothing to do with him or with the pain that was growing as blood began a slow trickle down his arm. The arrow was made of a straight stick, stripped of bark and fletched with goose feathers. Kenny had made dozens like it over the summer. *Kenny.* As he thought this, another hiss, another tremor, and an arrow struck the birch tree's trunk and bounced off, clattering against the boulder as it fell into the leaf litter at its base.

The raven had lifted itself into the air and flapped away even before the arrow reached the tree. Elijah slid quickly off the boulder and dropped to the ground away from the direction the arrows had come from. The arrow in his arm shook when he landed, sending pain through his arm, into his shoulder, even down his back. Kenny had put no tips on his arrows, had merely sharpened their shafts to fine points. Elijah ought to be able to pull it out. Leaning against the boulder, he gritted his teeth, took hold of the arrow by its fletching, and tugged. Pain washed over him as he pulled the arrow free, its shaft red with blood.

Had Kenny been aiming at him, he wondered, or at the raven? Raven, he decided. Did that mean, now that the raven had flown safely out of range, that Kenny would give up and go back to camp? Elijah listened, straining through the sounds of a summer forest to pick out anything that didn't belong. He heard the occasional rasp of a locust, the distant growl of thunder, and beneath them, coming not from outside but from within, the faint buzz of Kenny's presence. Blood welled slowly from the wound in his arm. He pulled off his T-shirt, doing his best not to move his arm in the process, and wrapped it as well as he could around the wound, tucking in the ends to hold it.

Then he heard the sound of Kenny moving, scuffling toward him through the leaves and undergrowth.

Enemy, Elijah thought. One thing certain, Kenny was not coming to offer help. Staying low to the ground, Elijah scrambled up the hill, keeping as much cover as possible between himself and his pursuer.

Rats, Kenny had thought when the arrow pierced Elijah's arm. He had not been aiming at the kid. Quickly he'd notched another arrow, taken aim at the bird on the branch of the birch tree, and let it fly. Almost as soon as the arrow left the bow, he saw that it too would miss. The bird was already taking off, as if it had seen the arrow and was moving—almost casually—out of its way. Elijah had slid down the other side of the boulder and disappeared. Kenny had to think what to do. The arrow was lodged in Elijah's upper arm. It wouldn't do any real harm there, he thought. The wound couldn't be too bad. It wasn't as if he'd killed the kid.

But what would Cassie say? He couldn't even say he'd been aiming at the stupid raven. She'd made it more than clear he wasn't to hurt that bird. As if something bad might happen if he did. Not to Elijah but to them. All of them. Some kind of black magic thing.

Even if Elijah didn't actually show up back at camp with one of Kenny's arrows sticking out of his arm, that wound was trouble. What would they think had happened to him? They'd know even if the kid couldn't tell them. You didn't get a wound like that falling off a rock.

Falling off a rock. Or a cliff. Kenny had come this way last winter when he was tracking that fox in the snow. Just over the next ridge the animal's tracks had run along the edge of a sheer drop and then angled down and around on a ledge too narrow for him to follow. The fox probably had a den somewhere among the broken faces of rock in the cliffside. The drop from the top had been a long one, scary enough that Kenny had stayed well back from the edge. What if Elijah were to fall from there? A person could die in a fall like that. And even if a person fell and only broke his leg, if nobody knew where he was he might not survive long enough to be rescued.

Slinging his bow over his shoulder, Kenny started toward the boulder where Elijah had been sitting. He made no effort to move quietly. He wanted Elijah to hear him coming. He wanted Elijah to run. He would follow, maybe loosing an arrow now and again, and move the kid toward that cliff. If he was lucky, Elijah might not see the cliff in time. He might fall over the edge all by himself. And if he didn't—well. If he didn't, Kenny might just give him a little help.

Elijah ran, scrambling down around rocks and up between the trees, tripping over roots and fallen limbs. Every step jolted his arm, sending pain down to his hand and up across his shoulders and into his neck. Twice Kenny shot again, the arrows going wide first to one side, then to the other.

When he was just about out of strength and breath, a stitch in his side contending for his attention with the pain in his arm, Elijah reached the top of a long ridge only to find himself at the edge of a sudden sharp drop. Full-size trees growing below reached their branches only a few feet over his head. Massive moss-covered boulders that had broken from the rock face were strewn on the slope below, thickly grown up with vines and young trees. There were plenty of places to hide down there, he thought, but he couldn't see a way to get to them.

As he bent over to ease the pain in his chest, Elijah's mind clicked in for the first time since he had begun to run. It was Kenny coming behind him, Kenny, who'd done everything he could all year to make Elijah's life miserable. Kenny, shooting arrows that could do real damage. *Enough*, Elijah thought. *Enough running.*

There was an old tree at the edge of the cliff, half its roots reaching out and down into space. Elijah sank to the ground at the base of the tree and leaned against its rough bark, his arm throbbing in time with the faster rhythm of his pounding heart. He would wait here. Kenny wouldn't be careful, would think his quarry was in hiding. Kenny wouldn't expect a fight.

Elijah took a deep breath and closed his eyes for a moment. He would have liked to quit hurting, to sink into a soft bed filled with pillows and drift away. There had been times before when he had felt like this, when the Man had beaten him bloody and he had curled up under the bush outside the apartment building, longing for his old bed with the quilt Mama Effie had made him, back home in Carolina. But this time he wouldn't run, wouldn't hide. This time would be different.

The buzz in his head grew louder, and he heard a crackling in the leaf litter on the other side of the tree trunk that alerted him an instant before Kenny struck him, tumbling him toward the edge of the cliff. Arms held him, jamming his wound against the hard ground so that pain went through him like a lightning bolt, unleashing a level of fury that blotted out everything except the determination to hurt back. With a strength he didn't know he had, Elijah wrenched free and threw Kenny off.

Before the other boy had a chance to scramble up, Elijah leaped on him, ignoring the flare of pain in his arm, and pinioned Kenny's arms against his sides, sitting on his middle so that he could only flail helplessly with his legs. The movement slid both of them closer to the edge of the cliff. Elijah jammed one foot against a tree root to stop their slide. As Kenny struggled beneath him, Elijah saw that if he grabbed for a low branch just above his head and kept his foot anchored, he could let go of Kenny's arms and, at the same moment shove with his free arm and his other leg to send Kenny over the edge. The image of what he could do unfurled itself with infinite clarity in his mind—Kenny's body sliding along the slanted rock and disappearing, disappearing.

Into Elijah's field of vision at that moment came the raven, landing on the tree whose root was bracing the two of them, and the image burst like a balloon. It was not something Elijah could do. Not even to Kenny. In the next instant Kenny had jerked himself free of Elijah's grip and flung himself onto him, wrapping his legs around Elijah's and kicking to dislodge Elijah's foot from the root. Elijah felt his sneaker slip, his body moving closer to the cliff. He found a rock with his other foot and pressed his heel hard against it, only to feel the rock break loose and plunge over the edge.

Raven, Elijah thought, sending a call to the bird as he

felt his legs go over into space. He scrabbled with both feet, trying to find a foothold. The crumbling edge of rock was pressing into his hips now. He made a mental image of the bird swooping on Kenny as he had seen ravens mob an eagle, diving and striking at its head and back.

Kenny released him suddenly. Elijah grabbed with his right hand for something to hold on to, his fingers closing around a vine. It came away in his hand. Before he could reach again, he felt Kenny's feet in their thick-soled hiking boots against his bare shoulders. Kenny was holding on to the tree with both hands, shoving downward with a strength impossible to resist. The skin of Elijah's chest scraped against rock and tree roots. He managed to grab a root as he felt himself going over the edge, his legs flailing uselessly against the slope of bare rock. The root held. The weight of his body pulled at his hand, and he could feel his fingers beginning to slip.

Then Kenny was standing over him, stomping his hand against the tree root. He could no longer distinguish between the pain in his hand, his chest, his arm. He felt his fingers let go. *Raven,* he thought as he slid downward a few feet against the rock face and over into space. He heard and felt his body colliding with tree branches on the way down, pain exploding in him like fireworks. Then there was a crashing jolt and darkness.

• • •

Cold on his cheek. On his eyelid, his nose, his forehead, his chest. It was raining. How could it be raining on his bed? Where was his quilt? He had to wake up. Had to tell Mama Effie that the roof was leaking. But something hurt too much. He wanted to go back to sleep. Thunder crashed. He would tell her after the storm. Now he needed to sleep.

Elijah shivered and reached for the covers. No covers. His teeth were chattering, making terrible noises in his head, noises that hurt his skull. He reached with his other hand, and a wave of pain washed over him. Cold. He was so cold. He had to get warm. With an effort, Elijah opened his eyes. He was not in his bed. Of course not. Above him he could see limbs and branches and a sky thick with clouds, darkening toward night. He could smell pines and the rich smell of wet earth. He wanted to shake his head, to clear it. But every movement hurt.

There was a sound off to the side, near his head. A sense of movement. He turned toward it and found himself staring into the bright eyes of the raven. It fluffed the feathers of its head and then smoothed them, making low, murmuring sounds deep in its throat. It lowered its head and then raised it, spreading the feathers of its shoulders and tail. *Raven.* Shivering, Elijah turned away from the bird, closing his eyes again, his chattering teeth making a painful drumming in his head. He remembered what had happened now—the arrow, Kenny, the struggle at the edge of the cliff. The raven had not defended him.

Thunder rumbled in the distance, so low, so far, that Elijah felt it through the ground beneath him more than he heard it. He opened his eyes again. It would be dark soon. The air was getting chilly. He dared not stay where he was, wet and half-naked, all night. He moved one leg and then the other, checking for broken bones. As much as his legs hurt, he could move them both, bend his knees. But when he flexed his ankles, pain shot through him again. His right ankle was probably sprained.

He tried sitting up, but the movement of lifting his head was like exploding a bomb in his skull.

Quork. The raven hopped closer, spreading its wings and bobbing its head.

Go away, Elijah thought at it.

Elijah gritted his teeth and rolled himself over on his right side, away from his bandaged arm, toward the raven. The bird raised its wings and jumped backward.

Slowly, trying not to jolt any part of his body, Elijah raised himself so that he was supporting his upper body on his right elbow. He scanned the ground around him, looking for some kind of shelter. In dreamtime he had lived the life of a fox, a weasel, a woodchuck. Shelter could be found almost anywhere if you knew what to look for and if you were willing to put out a little effort. Ahead of him were the boulders he had seen from above. The nearest was more than twenty feet away, an impossible distance. Even if he could get that far, there looked to be no place near it that would give him what he needed.

He turned to look in the other direction. And saw it. One huge slab of rock had come to rest on another, toppled against it and jutting out so that there was a triangular space between and beneath them. It was choked with brambles, a deeper shadow in the growing darkness. The space looked big enough for him to get into, even without any sort of digging, maybe even big enough to sit up in.

Pulling himself with his elbow, he dragged his body around until he was facing the rocks. Then he began moving. He reached with his elbow and then pulled, reached and pulled, pushing with his good foot, moving himself no more than a few inches at a time, through ferns and wet leaves and ground clutter, over rocks and tree roots and fallen branches. His body was shaken with waves of uncontrolled shivering, and it felt as if every part of him, every muscle and bone and bit of bare skin, was damaged somehow.

As he went, the raven hopped along the ground with him, staying close but no longer making any sound.

Elijah ignored it. When at last he reached the shelter, it was fully dark. No moon was visible overhead, no stars, and though the distant rumble of thunder had faded, the chill air was still thick and heavy. It could rain again in the night, Elijah knew.

He pushed his way through the tangle of brambles at the base of the rocks. The scratches the thorns made on his skin as he moved among them took his attention only for moments. Elijah was not sure there was room left in him for more pain.

When he was fully into the space, supported by his now-bleeding elbow and arm, Elijah found that the ground beneath the rocks was covered with a thick layer of pine needles and leaves. More important, it was dry. In the fully wet world, this small space was dry. If it did rain in the night, he would not get wet again.

But he was so cold he could hardly think. He had to have some sort of covering. Pine branches or ferns would make some cover, but he had no way to get them. He had only the bloody T-shirt that bound the wound in his arm. As gently as he could, he unwrapped the bandage. It was stuck to the wound, so that pulling it away was like tearing adhesive tape from an open sore. There was something to be said for hurting as much as he did, for going out to the very edges of pain. The only difference pulling the bandage away made was to move his attention from one part of his body to another.

When the shirt came free, the wound bleeding again, he managed to straighten out the damp shirt. But there was no way he could put it on. He would have to settle for pulling it over himself like a skimpy sheet and hoping his body heat would dry it out.

Elijah lay down, grateful for the pine needles, for the fact that the ground under him was level and dry. He let himself roll onto his back, holding his head up carefully until his body was settled and then letting it down as gently as he could. Even so, a bomb exploded inside his skull again as his head touched the ground. It was a small bomb, but it was more than enough.

He closed his eyes and slipped immediately into sleep.

"It's the worst possible time," Charles Landis complained to Cassie as they stood together on the porch the morning after Elijah had failed to come back to the cottage. "We'll have to postpone the operation if we don't find him today. I never should have listened to you about that boy."

Amber sat on the porch steps, hunched over her stomach in an effort to calm it. When Elijah wasn't back in time for dinner the night before, she had gone out looking for him, checking all the spots she and he had gone to on their nature walks. There had been no sign of him anywhere, and she'd realized with surprise that when the two of them had been together, Elijah had always gone where she wanted to go. She had never thought to let him do the choosing. And as often as he had gone off alone, she had never thought to ask him where he went, never followed him to see what his favorite places might be. In all the woods and mountains around them, inside Paradise Park and out, she knew of no special place to begin the search.

Mack had split the men into teams that morning and sent them out searching, but she had not been able to tell them anything that would help. It was as if she'd never thought of Elijah as a separate person, someone whose world, even if it was right there with theirs, might be very different.

"Does he swim?" her father was asking Cassie now. He gestured toward the lake. "You don't suppose he might have drowned—"

Cassie, her face creased with worry, shook her head. "He swims. And he's learned to paddle a canoe. But the canoes are here. More important, his raven's not. If Elijah had drowned, that bird would be somewhere close."

Charles Landis sighed. "At least the boy can't talk. You're sure of that?"

Cassie shrugged. "He hasn't said a word in more than a year."

Amber started to speak but then bit her tongue. If they knew Elijah could talk, it would change nothing except to make them all more upset than they were already. At least now they weren't thinking that Elijah might get out and tell someone what was going on at Paradise Park. The thought made her stomach clench even more tightly. Would he tell? Was he on their side, or had he been all this time just a prisoner, waiting for an opportunity to escape, to report them all to the men in the uniforms?

She couldn't believe it. Didn't want to. Still, in all the conversations they'd had, though she could see that he hated the way the world was every bit as much as she did, he'd never offered a word of agreement about the Militia's mission. He agreed about the changes they wanted to make, but he'd never agreed about the fight it would take to make them.

"I told Mack to have the men watch for the raven," Cassie said. "If they find the bird, they'll find Elijah."

"How could they know it's his?" Charles Landis asked. "Ravens all look alike."

"If it lets itself be seen, it'll be Elijah's."

Amber's father shook his head. "Tell me one more time this kid is worth it."

Cassie put both hands up to her face, rubbed her eyes, and sighed. "I can't be sure. I can only tell you what I feel. Wolves and ravens, ravens and wolves. He's important to us. If he weren't, he wouldn't be here."

"That's the point. He *isn't* here!"

"I know." With that, Cassie turned and went back inside.

Charles Landis looked after her, absently rubbing the wolf tattoo on the back of his hand. Then he turned and went down the porch steps, touching Amber's head as he went by. "Don't you have work to do in the garden today? No sense letting *everything* come to a standstill around here."

So Amber went to the garden. As she worked, hoeing weeds in the wet ground between the rows of corn and beans, she pictured Elijah out in the woods somewhere, soaked by the rain that had come and gone all night, chilled, maybe hurt. He wasn't on his way out to find civilization, she thought. If he'd wanted to try that, he could have gone anytime. There were no fences keeping him in, nothing except the miles of wilderness between them and the nearest usable, traveled road. And if he wasn't lost or hurt, he'd have come back, as he always had before. She knew enough about him to know he had no other place to go. Whether he agreed with everything the Militia stood for or not, Paradise Park was his only home.

She thought of Tondishi, of the dream that had proved her connection to Elijah, and wondered if she could use that connection somehow, if she could link her mind to him and find him, contact him at least. But she hadn't the first idea how to begin. *Elijah,* she thought, doing her best to project the thought out into the world around her. *Where are you?* There was no answer. Of course not. She hadn't really expected one.

Late in the afternoon when the last of the search parties had returned without having found a trace of boy or raven, she went to the computer room to try to lose herself in the research she'd been doing on food preservation. It didn't work. Fifteen minutes later she was in the tunnel, heading for the lodge. She had decided to ask Mack to let her go out with a search party tomorrow. She couldn't stand another day of not knowing and not doing anything to find him.

As she got to the bottom of the steps that led up to the lodge, Kenny was on his way down. The moment he saw her, he turned and started back up again.

Why would he be avoiding her? Unless he knew something he hadn't told anyone. "Wait!" she said, and bounded up the steps after him.

She caught him by the arm, and he swore at her as he tried to pull free. But she managed to hold on and twisted his arm behind his back. "Where's Elijah?" she said.

"How should I know?"

"That's what I want to find out. Where is he?"

Kenny kicked backward at her, but she moved out of the way in time to dodge his foot. "It's not my business to keep track of Cassie's pet retard," he said.

Amber pushed his arm higher up his back until he yelped. "I asked what you know about Elijah."

With a speed that surprised her, Kenny twisted his body, lashed a foot out between her legs, and knocked her off-balance. Before she could recover, he jerked himself free of her grip and punched her hard in the arm. Then he loped down the stairs and ran down the tunnel toward the computer room.

That punch, which she could already tell would leave her arm swollen and bruised, convinced Amber of two things. One was that he did know something about Elijah's disappearance that he wasn't telling. The other was that Kenny had gotten beyond her. She was still taller than he was, but she wasn't going to be able to intimidate him by force anymore. There was no way to find out what he didn't want to tell.

It was hot in his shelter. Elijah rubbed his eyes and turned to peer out into the daylight beyond the brambles. Daylight. The last time he looked it had been dark. He felt as if he was waking up from a long sleep, torn by nightmares. He didn't know how long, how many days, how many nights, he had been there. He could remember darkness and light, sweats that soaked his clothes and chills that forced him to huddle into himself under the flimsy cover of his filthy T-shirt, his good arm clasped around his knees. He thought there had been more rain, a storm, with lightning as well as thunder, and the wind so hard in the trees overhead that he had heard limbs crack and fall, crashing through branches, bringing more down with them.

He had stayed dry enough in his shelter, but rainwater had collected in depressions in the rock above. He remembered having lapped that water like a dog whenever he crawled out of his shelter to relieve himself. It was hard to believe there was anything for his body to eliminate. He had eaten nothing since his fall from the cliff but a handful of blackberries that he'd found on the brambles through which he had to move whenever he came or went.

His body, bruised and scraped, was now marked with red scratches where the thorns had torn his skin.

However long he had been here, he had drifted in and out of consciousness without regard for light or darkness, and his sleep, if sleep it was, had been torn by nightmares, nightmares full of ravens, full of wolves. Waking had offered little comfort. At least in the dreams he had been blessedly free from the pain that descended in all its force when he woke. In many of the dreams the raven had played a part but never defending him, never saving him.

Quork.

Elijah pushed himself up to a sitting position and peered out between the brambles. The raven peered in, brilliant sunlight showing up iridescent greens and blues in the black of its feathers. Elijah had not seen the bird except in dreams since the night he had dragged himself into his shelter. *Go! Leave!* He felt around him for something to throw at it, but there was nothing.

For a long time, eye to eye, neither moved. Then the raven stretched upward and pulled loose a blackberry Elijah had somehow missed. It held the berry in its beak, bobbing its head up and down, making chuckling sounds deep in its throat. Elijah understood its offer, wanted to reject it. But his body would not let him. He dragged himself closer and reached his hand gingerly between the brambles. The raven dropped the berry delicately into Elijah's open palm.

Elijah ate the berry, pressing it against the roof of his mouth with his tongue, letting the sweetness and the juice run down his throat. He would have liked to make it last forever, but it was gone with a chew and a swallow. The bird tipped its head and looked at him with one eye and then the other. Elijah turned away. If the raven wanted gratitude, it would have to look elsewhere.

He tested his swollen, discolored ankle, pushing his foot against the rock wall of his shelter. Pain shrieked up his leg. His stomach rumbled. The blackberry had wakened it to the need for food. Real food. Elijah remembered what he had thought about Kenny all that time ago, that he might prefer starvation to biting into a white, squirming grub. Elijah had no such problem. If he could get himself to a fallen tree, an old, rotting stump, he could use a stick to dig some out.

He dropped his T-shirt on the floor of his shelter and crawled out, blinking in the glare. The raven flew to the top of his rock shelter. It fluffed its head feathers, raised and then lowered its wings, its eyes focused intently on Elijah's face. Elijah dragged himself to his feet, keeping his weight off his right foot, to see if there was anything left of the puddles in the rock. He sucked up the last of the water, peed against the rock, then lowered himself carefully to the ground to begin the long crawl to the nearest rotting log.

As he moved, his teeth gritted against the pain, he thought that Amber had been right all along. You had to fight. What would have happened if he had fought Kenny from the beginning? Could he have beaten him at his own games? He didn't know. Kenny was bigger, stronger. But maybe he could at least have made the kid think twice about coming after him. He'd been blaming the raven all the time for not diving on Kenny, not driving him off. The bird was plenty big enough to have made a difference. But what had the raven done that Elijah himself hadn't been doing from the very beginning? Just staying out of the way.

When at last Elijah reached the moss-crusted log, its bark long gone, he found that the damp wood, honeycombed with tunnels and holes, crumbled away so easily that he could dig into it with his bare hands. Ants and beetles scurried away as he dug until he found the small white forms of larvae. He picked them out and, refusing to think, popped them into his mouth and swallowed.

When he had eaten all he could find, he sat with his back against the remains of the log, to rest. Getting here had taken all his energy. The sun was high now and getting hot. But it would be awhile before he could make the trek back to his shelter to get out of the sun. As he sat, his eyes closed against the glare, he remembered the moment when he'd known that he could push Kenny over the cliff, the moment when everything could have been different. In that moment he must have loosened his grip, given Kenny what he needed to get the upper hand. It was his own fault, then, that he was here. He hadn't been able to do what Kenny had done without a thought as soon as he had a chance.

Live. If that was still what he was supposed to do, Elijah wasn't sure he could do it. Would anyone find him here in time? He couldn't get back to Paradise Park on his own, or anywhere else for that matter, even if he had a place to go. But he knew that if he wanted to live, he was going to have to be willing to fight.

Charles Landis was the alpha wolf who led his pack. Ravens and wolves, wolves and ravens, Cassie had said they belonged together. If Elijah was to live, it would be with the pack. Kenny had a place with them. Elijah would find a place too.

Quork.

Elijah opened his eyes. The raven was standing on the rock that was Elijah's shelter. It launched itself into the air, circled once above Elijah's head, and then flew up over the cliff and disappeared.

Amber sat on the cottage porch, a glass of lemonade on the arm of her Adirondack chair, her bare feet resting on the porch railing, a book open in her lap. She was pretending to read. But her thoughts were, as they had been almost continuously for five days, on Elijah.

She had gone out with the O'Donnell brothers to look for Elijah for two days, until her father had told her she was more useful here. She had not minded so much by then, because the strain of searching had turned out to be almost worse than the strain of waiting. At first she'd thought that even if no one else could find him, she could somehow. Every rustle in the undergrowth, every movement she had caught out of the corner of her eye had sent her heart jolting with the possibility that it could be Elijah instead of a squirrel, a woodpecker, a snake slithering out of her way.

But Stephen had thought all along that Elijah was probably dead, so the search was worthless even if they found him. He'd say it every time they stopped for a break. Finally she'd begun to be afraid to look for fear of finding Elijah's body. Stephen had ridiculed both her insistence on calling Elijah's name as they went—"as if he could answer" and his brother's certainty that the boy was alive out there somewhere, lost and staying put till he was found.

"It's the sensible thing to do, and he's no dummy," Jack had said. "You can see it in his eyes, even if he can't talk. That's why we have to find him, why Mack's holding everything up till we do. If somebody else finds him, hikers or rangers or somebody, he could give us completely away. We haven't a clue how much he knows, and he doesn't have to talk to get the information across. He can read, so you know he must be able to write."

"Dead," Stephen had answered. "I'm right. You wait and see."

Finally last night Mack had agreed with Stephen and called off the search. It was dangerous country. There were plenty of streams and rivers where he could have drowned, plenty of peaks and cliffs he could have fallen from. Her father had agreed too. The boy was surely dead. It was time to get back to work. They had had to postpone their operation for almost a week now. There was no sense postponing any further.

But Amber refused to believe it. Even if she couldn't send her mind out to connect with him, she had a feeling that she'd know, somehow, if Elijah was gone. She'd sense it. There would be a hole, she thought, a hole she would feel in the middle of herself where the worry still kept her stomach clenched.

As for Cassie, Amber couldn't decide what Cassie believed. Amber had found her in the greenhouse this afternoon. When she'd walked in, Cassie had been moving along the table full of plants potted for winter growing, stroking a leaf here, straightening a stake there. Her mind had not seemed to be on what she was doing.

"Do you think Elijah might have gotten out to a road or one of the big trails, someplace where somebody could find him?" Amber had asked. She had been struggling between hoping that was what had happened, to be sure he was still alive, or being afraid if he got out, he'd tell about the Militia.

Cassie shrugged. "No way to know."

"You used to think the raven was like some kind of bodyguard."

"I used to think a lot of things." Cassie had looked at Amber then, her dark eyes troubled. "Look, Amber, I could have been wrong about him. I haven't lived with Indians since I was ten years old, as your dad keeps reminding me. What do I know about the old ways? Maybe it was just wishful thinking. Signs and symbols and healing. Where's the proof of any of it?" She pulled a twist tie from her shirt pocket and began tying a drooping cherry tomato vine to its support. "If the old ways were so good, why would Indians be living the way they are now?"

"Do you think he's dead?"

The tomato vine broke under Cassie's fingers. She looked down at it and cursed under her breath. Then she tossed the broken piece on the floor. "Ask Mack and your father. Not me." She had not spoken of Elijah since.

Amber couldn't remember the last time she'd cried. Not since the night her mother died probably. But this morning when she woke up, she'd found her cheeks wet with tears. Whatever dream she'd been having, she knew it was about Elijah.

The raven came so suddenly, wind whistling through its wing feathers as it dropped down out of the sky, that Amber jumped, knocking her glass of lemonade to the floor as she jerked her feet back. The bird landed on the porch railing where her feet had been, folded its wings, and looked directly at her, making no sound.

Amber stood up, and the book fell to the floor. Though the bird raised its wings in alarm and uttered a sharp, rasping cry, it didn't fly away. "Wait here," she told it, feeling like a fool for talking to a bird and even more of a fool for what she was thinking. "I've got to get shoes."

In her room Amber hurriedly changed from the

shorts she'd been wearing into jeans and pulled on socks and hiking boots. She didn't know where they were going or how long it would take, but if it got dark before she got back, it would also get chilly. She grabbed a flashlight and hooked it to her belt, pulled a sweatshirt jacket out of her drawer, and tied it around her waist by the sleeves.

She dug through the crate that held Elijah's few clothes. He'd been wearing jeans and a T-shirt when he disappeared, and he might need something warmer too. In the kitchen she found a couple of PowerBars and stuffed them, along with two bottles of water, the first-aid kit from the drawer by the sink, and Elijah's sweatshirt, into a daypack she'd snatched from the hook in the hall.

Outside, the raven was still where it had been when she left. So maybe she wasn't so crazy after all. "Let's go," she told it. "Just remember I can't fly."

She didn't wait for the bird. She ran down the porch steps and started toward the lake. With a clatter of wings the raven rose into the air, swooped low over her head, and then veered off around the corner of the cottage. Amber changed direction and followed it into the woods.

When the bird landed on a tree with roots dangling over the edge of a cliff, Amber stood for a moment, looking down. The bird made a nasal, honking sound and floated down to land on a low branch of a tree at the base of the cliff. "I can't get there from here," she called down to it, as if it could understand her words. The sun was hot and bright, and Amber was sweating from the climb to the cliff's edge. She had no idea how far the raven was taking her or whether it was really leading her to Elijah. But she'd come this far; there was no point stopping.

She walked along the edge of the cliff and came to a place where a huge piece of the rock edge had broken partially loose, its far edge almost resting against a pine tree rooted below. She could use the tree like a ladder, Amber thought. She scrambled across the rock and then, holding the tree trunk, stepped down onto the nearest branch. From there it wasn't hard to move down branch by branch, her hands getting sticky with pitch, until she reached the stubs of dead branches that she didn't trust to hold her. She dropped the rest of the way, only about ten feet, landing in the soft bed of needles at its base.

The raven was perched on a shrub nearby, waiting for her. It flew, and she followed until it landed atop a pair of boulders, one tipped against the other. When she came close, the bird didn't fly again. Instead it ruffled its feathers, fluffed its head, and made a series of long calls.

After a moment Amber saw a movement among the blackberry brambles at the base of the boulders. An arm appeared, and then Elijah partly crawled, partly dragged himself from the space between the rocks. She saw that the first-aid kit was not going to be enough.

Amber gave Elijah the PowerBars and one of the bottles of water, telling him to go slowly with both. He ignored her advice. While he ate, stuffing big pieces of the bars into his mouth and washing them down with the water, she looked at his arm and his ankle and determined she could do nothing about the ankle and hardly anything about the arm. The arm injury was a puzzle. It seemed clear that Elijah had fallen from the cliff—he had bruises everywhere—but she couldn't imagine what could have punctured his arm like that. A puncture it clearly was, all the way through the muscle of his upper arm. Pus was draining from it on both sides. His arm was inflamed all the way around the wound, and it wasn't the heat of the sun that was making his skin hot to the touch. He had a fever. The wound needed to be cleaned and bandaged, and he needed an antibiotic besides.

Amber hoped the infection was something they could treat at Paradise Park. There was no way her father would let Elijah get out to a hospital.

"Did you try healing yourself?" she asked him. "Like you did with my knee that time?" Elijah shook his head. "Well, why not? It worked on me."

"I was sick. Too sick to think of it. Anyway, I don't know if it would work doing it to myself."

"Seems to me it would be worth a try! I'll put antiseptic ointment on your arm and bandage it for the trip back. This is going to hurt," she warned him.

"Everything hurts," he said. And then he smiled.

For the first time since he'd disappeared, Amber found herself smiling too. *Thank you*, she thought in the direction of the raven, which was watching every move she made.

"Now," she said, when the bandaging was done, "we have to figure out how to get you back." It was obvious they couldn't take the direct way. They wouldn't be able to get up the cliff. They'd have to go around it; that meant there could be miles more to walk. They'd have to find the overgrown road that had once been Paradise Park's main entrance. From the look of Elijah's ankle, swollen to the size of a softball, he wouldn't be able to put his weight on it.

"The survival stuff I got off the nets told how to make a litter," she told him. "You string vines between two big branches to make a sort of stretcher. Then I'm supposed to be able to drag you back." She pulled the Swiss Army knife from her pocket. "This is fine for the vines, but I don't know how I'd cut branches. Maybe I can find some on the ground."

Elijah pointed at the sun, which was well past the middle of the sky. "By the time you're done, it'll be getting dark."

So Amber decided on the simplest, most direct way. Elijah's injuries were diagonal—left arm, right ankle. She got him to his feet and put his good arm around her shoulder, her left arm around his waist. "You can hop on your left leg. We'll take it slow," she told him. "If you get tired, we'll take a break. It's too hot for the sweatshirt I brought you now, but if you get chilled, let me know that too."

Amber wasn't certain she could find her way. The cottage was on the opposite side of the lake from the rest of Paradise Park, and she had never gone far into the woods behind it. But a minute or two after they started, Elijah hopping at her side, the raven flew over them and began leading them, the way it had led her to Elijah's shelter. His "den" was how Amber thought of it. She had braved the brambles to crawl inside before they started back, and it had reminded her of the den of an animal, snug and dry. If he hadn't found it, she thought, Mack would have been right. Elijah would surely have been dead by now.

As they moved along, struggling over creeks and up slopes that felt too steep to manage at all, Amber told Elijah of the search parties that had been looking for him. And the calling off of the search when Mack decided he couldn't have survived. "Your name ought to be Lazarus," she told him. "Do you know that story? Lazarus?"

Elijah nodded. "I used to read the Bible a lot."

"I never read it. But I heard the story a long time ago. Back before—" She paused. She had never told Elijah about her mother's death. She would someday, she thought. "Back when I was really little. I went to Sunday school then, and they used to tell us Bible stories."

Elijah tugged at the sleeve of her T-shirt. "Break," he said. She settled him on the ground, his back against a fallen tree, and then sat next to him on the trunk. He closed his eyes, and she watched his chest rise and fall as he took long, deep breaths. He was so skinny she thought she could see his heart beating under his ribs. The raven flew back to them and landed nearby.

Amber was glad Elijah needed the break. She was more tired than she'd thought. *It's too bad that Lazarus thing is just a story*, she thought. *Too bad nobody can really bring people back after they die*. After a while she checked the angle of the sun and urged Elijah to his feet again. He looked awful, but she needed to balance his need for rest with their need to get back before dark.

The raven led them to a place where the ground sloped up to the long ridge of rock that had formed the cliff. Here it was much lower, no more than a series of ledges. Amber could hoist Elijah up from below, then scramble up herself. When they reached the top, they sat on the last ledge to get their breath, and the raven spiraled up into the sky until it was far above them, gliding in huge circles. "I wish I could do that," Amber said.

"You can," Elijah said.

"Oh, sure. Just leap off here and fly."

Elijah shook his head. "Close your eyes," he said.

Amber closed her eyes. At first she saw only darkness, spangled with splotches of yellow orange, the afterimages of the sun. Then she seemed to see the ledge they were on, as though she were standing on its edge, poised for flight. As if in a dream, she imagined herself taking off, stretching her arms and leaping out onto the air. Suddenly it felt real. She felt the sensation of wind in her face, the way her arms, her wings, could control her glide, tilting slightly this way or that, moving a few feathers here, a few feathers there. Below, the forest sloped away, and she could see the whole land spread out beneath her. Off to the left she could even see the open space in the trees that was Paradise Park, the lake glittering in the sun, the buildings scattered around its eastern end. She would have liked to stay that way the rest of the afternoon, gliding above the mountains in the wind.

But she shook herself out of the fantasy. "Incredible!"

she said, wondering what Elijah had had to do with it. She dug out the second water bottle. After drinking a little, she handed it to Elijah for his turn. He smiled his thanks. "Time to get going," she told him. "We can't just loll around in comfort like this all day."

It was dusk when they reached the crumbling stone gates that had once been the main entrance to Paradise Park. Amber was carrying Elijah piggyback now, wearing her daypack against her chest. She was so grateful to see the gates she'd have shouted if she'd had a scrap of energy left. Or the breath to shout. "It's only about a quarter of a mile to the lodge now," she said. When the sun had slipped behind the mountains and the air cooled, she had put her sweatshirt jacket on Elijah, because it was easier than putting his own on him over his head. She wished she'd brought along another. His was too small for her. She was hot from the exertion of carrying him, but her bare arms were cold, and her shirt was damp and chilly against her skin.

Elijah had told her during one of their breaks what had happened to his arm. And he'd told her about the scuffle at the cliff's edge. He'd fought back this time, the way she'd told him to. It made her feel as if she was as guilty of what had happened to him as Kenny. It was during the fight that Elijah had gotten too close, had rolled off and down. If he hadn't fought back, the accident wouldn't have happened. Well, she'd more than made it up to him, getting him back here, she thought. She hoisted him higher on her back and struggled over a tree that had fallen across the road. Then she thought about the fact that Kenny could have told them from the beginning exactly where Elijah was. Kenny had been willing to let Elijah die. She didn't know how Elijah could protect himself from him in the future. But at least for now it probably didn't matter much. Kenny was bound to be in big trouble, with Cassie, anyway, when she saw Elijah's wound. Maybe that would scare him off for a while.

Amber saw the lodge ahead at last. The raven was perched on its roof, and Cassie and her father were at the door. She breathed a deep sigh of relief and heard Elijah's, like an echo, in her ear.

Elijah and Amber had been fed and Elijah's ankle and arm wound soaked and bandaged. Ham had sent over some leftover antibiotics from the time he'd cut himself on a bandsaw and the wound had become infected. Elijah was sleeping now, tucked safely into his cot. Kenny had been banished from the cottage, sent to bunk in the men's quarters.

"It couldn't suit him better," Amber complained as she and Cassie put away the medical supplies and washed the dishes. "He'll think he's a real soldier now. One of the men. It's like a reward instead of a punishment."

"I don't think your father wanted to punish him. More likely he wanted to get Kenny away from me before I did. The only good thing Charles sees in your bringing Elijah back is knowing for certain that he isn't out there telling anybody anything. Your father would have been just as happy if you'd found Elijah's body. He's never believed the boy can be any use to us."

"But you were right about the raven. It led me to him, and it led us back here."

Cassie nodded. "I guess there's something to be said for the old ways after all. But it'll take more than that to convince Charles."

When Amber went to bed, she lay for a long time staring up at the roof beams. Had Elijah somehow *sent* her that fantasy about flying, or had she done it herself? Could she do it again? It had felt as if, for just that little bit of time, she had become the raven, as if her mind had been behind its eyes. She closed her eyes and concentrated on the image of the bird sitting as she had last seen it, on the lodge roof in the dwindling light. She took a long breath, held it a moment, and then slowly let it out. Then another. All the while she kept the image of the raven in her mind as best she could.

Quork.

Imagining she'd heard a raven call, Amber drifted into sleep.

By the next day the swelling in Elijah's ankle was nearly gone. When Cassie had Amber change the bandage on his arm, they saw that the wound had stopped draining. The inflammation was almost gone, and his fever had lifted. "You've been working on yourself, haven't you?" Amber asked him.

Elijah nodded and grinned.

"Have you ever seen anything get that much better that fast?" Amber asked Cassie. "Don't you think that would be enough to convince Dad that Elijah has something the Militia could use?"

Charles Landis had ordered Elijah confined for the time being. The men were installing a perimeter alarm system to alert them to the approach of a stray hiker or someone more threatening. It would work to let them know if someone was moving out of their territory too, and he didn't want the boy out wandering until it was finished. Cassie had told him it would be at least a week before Elijah would be up and around. And another week before he could get far enough away to trip any alarms. It wasn't going to be anywhere nearly that long.

"Listen, Cassie. The Cadre can't risk going to hospitals. When Ham hurt his hand, we waited almost too long before anybody drove him up to that urgent care center by the border. The doctor there said he'd come close to losing his thumb. If Elijah had put his hands on that right at the start, Ham might not have needed a doctor at all. That's what Elijah can do for us."

Cassie nodded. "Charles is due back in Albany tonight," she said. "But I'll have him look at Elijah's wounds before he goes." She turned to Elijah and looked into his eyes, her face serious. "Would you do that if we needed you? Would you help us?"

Elijah's eyes moved to Amber and back to Cassie. He nodded.

HIGH FRONTIER
SCHOOL LIBRARY

Alone at the cottage, Elijah sat in the big chair with his foot propped on a pile of cushions. His ankle and arm ached, but nowhere nearly as badly as when the throbbing had wakened him from sleep just before dawn. That was when he'd tried Amber's idea, using what he had learned of Taryn's healing. He had rested one hand on the bandage on his arm, keeping it there till the heat built up and gradually faded away again. Then he'd pulled his ankle up so that he could reach it with both hands and had done the same thing again. Little by little the pain had quieted from a scream to a whisper.

When Amber hurt her knee, he had known that he could help, had offered it almost instinctively. Why had he not thought he could do the same thing for himself? It would have made the last few days bearable. Perhaps he could even have made himself well enough to find his own way back.

But as he thought of it, he knew he wouldn't have wanted it that way. He had learned something important since yesterday, something more important than the fact of connections. Amber cared about him, cared enough to find him and bring him back. It was almost like having family again. The start of family.

The others had searched for him only to protect themselves, the same reason Kenny had wanted him dead. But all that would change. He would do what Cassie and Amber wanted him to, use whatever healing he could manage for the good of Charles Landis's pack. And he would become one of them the way he had been one of the Ark family—separate but connected. If that was the way it was in the wild, ravens with wolves, each offering the other something they needed, that was the way he'd work it here. He would always have to watch his back, aware that Kenny would be looking for any chance to hurt him again. He would dodge, if he could, stay out of his way. But if necessary, now, he would fight back. As hard as he needed to fight.

The raven was nearby, he knew, had stayed in a tree near the cottage all night and all day. Maybe in some way it had been better that the bird had not protected him from Kenny. He wondered if it knew that. Something had changed for Elijah over these last awful days. Something outside and something inside.

part three

wolf pack

>Path:
>Laurel.grt.com!netnews.upenn.edu!crabapple.srv.cs.
>smu.edu!looking!bass!clarinews
>From: clarinews@clarinet.com (AP)
>Message-ID: <terrorismUR237_eb6@clarinet.com>
>Date: Wed, 03 July 02 18:14:23 EDT
>ALBANY, NY (AP) At 4:30 PM today simultaneous
>bomb blasts brought down towers carrying high-
>tension electric wires into and out of this capital city.
>Eight towers, strategically located in a ring around
>the city, were destroyed within a five-minute period,
>blacking out electrical service to thousands of
>customers.
>   The following message, which includes a quotation
>from the Declaration of Independence, was found at
>the site of one of the bomb blasts. "'Whenever any
>form of government becomes destructive of [life,
>liberty, and the pursuit of happiness], it is the right
>of the people to alter or to abolish it. . . .' We the
>people hereby alter. The next step will be to abolish."
>   This is the second time in six weeks a bombing has
>seriously affected New York's capital city. On May 12
>the target was a central telephone switching station.
>That bombing, which took place at 3 A.M. EDT, put
>out telephone service to much of the city.
>   "These strikes, like similar others in recent years,

>appear to be the work of domestic terrorists," said
>Governor Merrick, from his vacation home in the
>Hudson Valley. "Our antiterrorist task force is at
>work, and I can assure the citizens of the state of
>New York that the perpetrators of these attacks will
>be found and brought to justice."
>   The governor dismissed the suggestion that recent
>bombings could be linked to the infamous Northway
>bombing of August 2000. "The perpetrators of that
>horror are on death row. The Northway bombing was
>the brainchild of a mass murderer, designed to kill
>as many human beings as possible. Subsequent
>bombings have been directed against infrastructure
>rather than people. There is no reason to suspect a
>connection. However, we are working with the Royal
>Canadian Mounted Police to determine whether
>there is a connection between these events and
>several recent infrastructure strikes in Canada."

YEAR TWO—JULY

Elijah climbed through the wet forest, heading for his boulder. It had become a kind of refuge, now that Kenny knew better than to try to hurt him. And just now he needed refuge. All morning he had felt a growing sense of threat that he couldn't pinpoint, couldn't figure out. A storm had blown up after breakfast, thunder and lightning like a war raging, wind lashing the trees, rain pounding so hard it seemed as though the whole of Paradise Park was sitting under a waterfall. But it wasn't that he had been feeling, fearing. The storm was gone now, and still the threat continued to grow.

Coming out into an open space between the trees, he saw a trio of ravens circling overhead. He sent a mental greeting, and one of them broke away from the formation to swoop down and land on a dead, dripping branch in a pine tree directly in front of him. It erected the feathers of its head and shoulders, then bent its head and strutted back and forth on the branch, making gentle knocking sounds. It was the friendliest of the young birds that had come to Paradise Park in the spring to join the first. This one, easily recognizable by a single white feather on one wing, was female. It wasn't possible to tell a raven's sex by looking, but Elijah knew it the way he knew much else about these birds, simply because he knew. He had long since given up wondering how that happened.

Ravens didn't sing, but so varied were the soft and crooning syllables she uttered now that he felt, as he often felt with her, sung to, comforted. *Don't worry,* she seemed to be crooning. *Everything will be okay.*

The raven ended her song with a bell-like gonging note, shook her feathers, and launched herself from the pine, her great wings moving with ease and grace to lift her into the air. He stood for a moment, watching as she flew up to join the others. The three of them began a display of aerial acrobatics then, circling, diving, rolling in the air, spiraling upward in formation so tight it seemed they must collide, then breaking away to dive separately, their wings folded, toward the tree line. There they suddenly opened their wings and flew toward one another as if in a game of chicken, veering away at the last moment. They seemed to be celebrating the end of the storm. As the thought came into his mind, the birds completed an upward spiral and flew off toward the west, each dipping a wing as they went. It was a signal that sometimes meant hello, sometimes, as now, good-bye.

He went on walking up the hill to the cluster of boulders that included his own. Almost eleven, he was taller now than when he came here first, no longer needed the footholds for climbing. He could have vaulted onto his boulder easily, but his usual perch had become a puddle in the rain. He leaned against the damp rock instead, feeling the security of its solid presence, listening to the rain drip from the trees when they moved in the wind.

The threat he was feeling was not from the Militia to him. In the year since Amber had come to find him, he had made himself a place with the wolf pack, a place so secure that even Kenny, son of the alpha wolf, dared not challenge it. His place had not been won, as Amber and Cassie had expected, by his ability to heal, though he had done some of that, but by the gift for working with computers that he had discovered in the computer center at the Ark.

One day when Cassie and Duane Bruder, who knew more about computers than any of the others, were trying unsuccessfully to repair a crash that had taken down their netsite, Elijah had offered to help. It was the first time he had spoken to anyone but Amber, so at first they were more interested in the mere fact of his voice than in what he had said. But when he at last persuaded them to let him sit down at a keyboard, the speed with which he solved their problem had changed everything. The next time Charles Landis came to Paradise Park, Cassie asked Elijah to demonstrate what he could do. He did it by going into the Cadre's system and making changes that simplified and streamlined what they were already doing and opened possibilities they had never considered.

From that day on Elijah had been the Cadre's computer tech. Within a week Cassie had understood that his silence and withdrawal had not been caused by autism. She expanded his homeschool program to include much of the same on-line course work Kenny and Amber were doing, and he soon caught up with Kenny in most of it. After that, he had been accepted as one of the pack, treated much the same way as any of the others. His life had become full of activity, troubleshooting in the computer room, working outside in the gardens, helping the O'Donnells with the kitchen work, or working at a computer on math or history, writing or science.

Working with the men of the Militia, he had come to know them. As he did, his fear of them gradually dissolved. He didn't agree with everything they believed, everything they wanted to do, but they were not monsters. All the time he'd been mute they had treated him as if not speaking meant that he couldn't hear. Conversations they would not have had in front of Amber or Kenny they'd had freely when Elijah was present. Even after he had begun to speak, he used his voice so seldom that the men's habit persisted. They talked to one another as they worked as if he weren't there.

Most of their talk was not about the Militia's mission or its philosophy. It was casual talk about their lives: the O'Donnell brothers' growing up on a farm in Iowa, Duane Bruder's high school job at his grandfather's lumberyard, Ham's constant worry about his mother, who was sick with cancer.

He began to understand why each of them had joined Landis's war. The farm in Iowa had been taken by the banks, and Stephen and Jack's father had shot himself to death the day it was sold at auction. Bruder's Lumberyard closed when a super home and hardware store moved into town and took away its business. Duane's father and grandfather had eventually gone to work at that store, but Duane had found the Militia instead. Ham's mother couldn't afford the medical care she needed because the company she worked for had canceled its pension and health insurance plans. All the men had enemies, and they were the enemies the Wolf had created the Militia to fight. Mack had left college to join a guerrilla group in Central America. He never talked about his reasons, but Elijah could feel the anger that still raged in him. He too was surrounded by enemies.

Virgil was different. He talked as much as or more than any of the others, but his stories were all about women. He told about the girls he'd dated in high school, about the women he was dating now, none of whom knew about the others, the ones he intended to visit if Landis ever gave them a weekend off. To hear him tell it, there was no female under the age of forty in upstate New York who could resist his charms. The others rolled their eyes at one another over his stories, but they let them pass without challenge. Maybe, Elijah thought, Virgil thought being in the Militia would help him make his fantasies real.

Today the men's talk had been all business. The operation they were getting ready for was meant, Mack said, to come close on the heels of the bombing of the electrical towers, to keep building pressure on the state and its antiterrorist force. Elijah didn't know what the target was; that was the sort of information shared only in the War Room. He did know, though, that like the two most recent bombings, this one would be a joint operation between the Militia and its new allies on both sides of the Canadian border.

The alliances had been Mack's idea, created to allow the Militia to make more strikes across a wider territory, increasing the pressure while spreading the responsibility, to create confusion for the authorities. The Wolf,

Elijah knew, didn't like the alliances, but he had made no move to stop them. He was busy in Albany and more and more in Washington, doing the political work that could move the system from the inside, as he said. He came less and less often to Paradise Park. Mack was the one who was mostly running things now.

But Landis was due to come in later that day. A year ago, just knowing that he was coming would have been enough to account for Elijah's growing sense of threat, to send him out here to his refuge.

A breeze blew through the trees now, sending a chilly shower down on Elijah, as he stood against the boulder. He ran a hand over his hair, brushing the moisture away. This feeling he was having was more than the coming of the Wolf. Something bad was moving ever closer to them. Ever closer to him.

Everything will be okay, the raven had assured him. Elijah didn't believe it.

Amber sat between Elijah and Kenny at one of the long tables, picking at her grilled cheese sandwich. All morning she'd felt as if she was coming down with something. A stomach virus maybe. When it first started, she had been in the computer room, working on a set of algebra problems while Kenny, next to her, muttered and cursed about whatever project it was Cassie had given him to do. "It's summer!" he'd complained at one point, pushing his chair away from his workstation. "The least she could do is let up on us during the summer! Other kids don't have school every single day of their lives! It's a power trip, that's what it is. When Dad gets here, I'm going to talk to him about it."

After a few minutes he'd gone back to work, but the griping and moaning continued. Hoping it was only having to listen to Kenny that was making her stomach clench and her head ache, Amber had finally fled the room and gone looking for Cassie to see if there was any other job she could do till she felt better. She had passed Elijah on her way, helping Ham and Duane redo the caulking in the fiberglass panels that lined the tunnel. He had looked up as she went by, and when their eyes met, it seemed almost as if her headache clamped down even harder.

Now, as Elijah ate his barbecued beef sandwich next to her, she felt herself getting sicker. If she didn't know better, she might have thought there was some connection between Elijah and how she was feeling. Mack came in with Virgil and a man she had never seen before. The man, squarely built, with a nose that had been broken, a brown buzz cut, and tattoos on both arms, was talking with the others as he walked toward the food line.

It must be the man Virgil had brought in that morning before the storm hit, she thought. He was supposed to help with the new operation. A member of the White Nation, Cassie had told her he was. Cassie hadn't even tried to conceal her contempt for the group this man belonged to. "Imagine calling themselves the White Nation, as if they created it, as if they owned it. There wouldn't even *be* a nation if it weren't for all the non-white people who helped make it happen. Let alone the Indians who were here to start with!"

Cassie hated the idea of joining forces with people whose beliefs and philosophies she disagreed with so fundamentally, and Amber had a pretty good idea that her father hated it too. But Mack insisted that it made strategic sense. Whatever the other groups believed, whatever they stood for, the actions they were willing to take were the same as the Militia's. Much more could be accomplished by several groups working together than by one working alone, and it was better to have them working with the Militia, where Mack and Landis could at least maintain some control.

Amber watched the man as he filled his plate, Ham in line in front of him, Virgil behind. White Nation or not, he looked no different from any of the others. He could be one of the regular Militia who had come to join the Cadre in preparation for the next operation.

She took a bite of her sandwich, and without warning a wave of nausea hit her, making her gag, just as Elijah jerked and knocked over his glass. Milk spread across the table and began dripping onto her lap.

Elijah had never seen the man who came in with Mack and Virgil before. He noticed the rattlesnake tattooed up the man's arm from his elbow, disappearing under the sleeve of his T-shirt, and wondered what the snake's head looked like. Probably its mouth was open, showing fangs, maybe dripping poison. It was the sort of tattoo many of the men chose, as if an image on their skin could prove their power to the world, warn people away the way the snake's rattle did. Elijah stared hard at the man, wondering what sorts of fangs he might have, what sort of poison.

Elijah swallowed the bite of barbecue in his mouth and was about to take another when the familiar sinking sensation overtook him and he felt himself slip out of his own consciousness. He was looking, suddenly, through a different set of eyes, the eyes of the man with the snake tattoo.

Such a thing had never happened with a person before, and it took Elijah a moment to orient himself to the streams of sensation and thought that moved simultaneously through the man's mind. It was like tuning between stations on a radio or moving through layers of thin fabric.

There was hunger, focused on the smell of barbecue coming from the food line; there was the sound of Virgil's voice, advising him to avoid the coleslaw; there was the man's own voice saying that he'd never been partial to coleslaw, a statement Elijah recognized as a lie, told with easy and conscious intent. Coleslaw, especially with barbecue, was in fact a favorite. Images of the taste danced at the edges of awareness so that his mouth watered. The man's fleeting thought about his lie was that it was a sacrifice to miss one of his favorite combinations of flavors. But it was easier for people to trust someone who seemed very like themselves. The more like them, the more trustworthy. Virgil didn't like coleslaw, so coleslaw was out.

Beneath all the rest of the feelings, thoughts, images that filled the man's body, Elijah recognized the tension he himself had been feeling as he sat at his computer that morning, as if he had absorbed it even before he had seen the man, before he had joined consciousness with him. The tension was now tinged with an edge of excitement as thoughts tumbled in his mind. The man needed to remember every detail he had heard in the meeting, every detail of this camp that none of them had known existed. He'd been blindfolded during the jolting ATV trip in, but the place would be easy enough to spot from the air. He had personally found what had to be the center of the terrorist network!

Won't that prick of a Tredwell be blown away to learn that Charles Landis is the head of it all? Tredwell calls Landis the voice of moderation. So much for moderation! Landis himself was coming in this afternoon for a meeting. Landis was no fool, and he'd be especially on guard interacting with someone from another group. *Have to watch myself with a man like that. It'll be the toughest role I've played since the FBI sent me to join the White Nation.*

Then, without warning, Elijah found himself back in his own body, so suddenly that he jerked with the sensation and knocked over his milk. As Amber reached for napkins to sop up the spill, Elijah sat like a stone, putting it all together. The snake man was Charles Landis's worst nightmare, the reason no Militia member was allowed into the Cadre, allowed even to visit Paradise Park until he'd been a member in good standing for at least three years. The man was a spy, a government infiltrator. He had wormed his way into the White Nation, and his presence there had led him here, thanks to Mack's policy of making alliances.

What had just happened was no normal dreamtime experience, Elijah realized. It had a purpose—definite, immediate, and important. He could feel its energy filling him, alerting him, sharpening his awareness. The survival of the wolf pack depended on what he did now. If he did nothing, said nothing, Paradise Park would be surrounded by government men as soon as the snake man got away to report what he'd learned here. They'd close the place down, put Landis in jail. And what would happen to the rest of them? Cassie? Amber? Himself?

"Where is he now?" Charles Landis was sitting across the table from Cassie in the cottage kitchen, turning a beer bottle absently in his hands.

"Upstairs reading. Do you want me to call him down?"

Landis shook his head. "I don't think I want to know any more than what you've told me. The kid read the man's mind?"

"That's what he says. Amber believes him, and so do I. It's no wonder they had him in a mental institution. This culture doesn't have any way to account for what he is, what he can do. A hundred years ago my people would have recognized it. And they'd have known what to do with him, how to teach him to use it."

"If he can read minds, how much teaching does he need?"

"Probably a lot. And from what I've seen of the way he learns everything else, he'd be some shaman's star pupil. I've told you, since I set him to learning on the nets, he's gone beyond Kenny in math, and Amber can barely stay ahead of him. And you know about him and computers. I thought maybe it was the autism. But he isn't autistic."

"The CIA worked with psychics back in the seventies. They said that psychic stuff didn't work."

Cassie just looked at him. "Since when does Charles Landis believe the CIA?"

"All right, all right. But I'm not altogether sure I want a mind reader around." Landis rubbed his face with both hands. "It's creepy. And maybe dangerous. You know how important it is to be able to keep secrets."

"What happened today was the first time with a person, he says. Usually he does it with animals."

"He reads the minds of animals."

Cassie shrugged. "It's more like joining consciousness with them, he says. Shamans call it shape shifting. He calls it dreamtime. But they aren't dreams. He's awake when it happens. He says it happened today without his intending it. Maybe because the information is so important. Like the way a man can sometimes get the strength to lift a car off his child. It's something he couldn't do except at that moment, when his child's life depends on it. Our lives depend on this. Ravens and wolves. I told you he was important to us some way."

"I know, I know. If he didn't intend this, what can the kid do when he *does* intend it?"

Cassie shrugged. "I doubt if even he knows. Amber thinks he can *send* as well as receive. She thinks he showed her how it feels to be a raven once, how it feels to fly. And he's been doing it lately with math problems if he's already done them and she gets stuck."

"Telepathic cheating?"

"He doesn't send answers. He sends process, principles, so she can do the problems herself. She says it's not like she hears his thoughts in her head. But when she's been stuck on a problem for a while and she starts to get upset about it, he'll just look at her sometimes, and the information will be there in her head, like remembering."

Landis frowned. "I'm not sure I believe any of this. But if there's even a chance he's right about this guy, I have to act." He leaned forward. "Is he *right*?"

"He thinks he is. And that's enough for me."

Landis checked his watch. "I'm supposed to meet with the men in fifteen minutes. I won't tell Mack about this. He's already defensive about these alliances he's created. I'll just go along with whatever he's got planned, and then do what I need to do." He drained his beer and stood up. "If the kid's made a mistake, it's going to be a costly one—for the White Nation and maybe for us."

"And if he hasn't—"

"That's why I'm listening to you, Cassie. That's why I'm listening."

Elijah was clearing the breakfast dishes from the tables the next morning, as the men talked over their coffee. The experience he had had the day before was not happening again. The infiltrator, whose name was Henkel, was telling Ham, Virgil, and Duane about what he planned to do later that day when he got back to Malone. Elijah could see that he was trying to impress them. But that was nothing more than observation. He was as shut out from the man's mind as anyone in the room.

"There's a couple of sisters, see, twins," Henkel was saying. "Identical redheads. You never saw anything like these two. Built? I mean to tell ya! They hang out at a bar I go to." He pointed his rattlesnake tattoo. "They dig my rattler. Thanks to this guy, I mostly leave that place with one of those girls at my side." He laughed. "Sometimes both of them."

"What are they, pros?" Virgil said.

"Heck, no, they're not pros. Bud Henkel doesn't pay for what he wants."

"What bar is this?" Virgil asked.

"Look out," Ham said. "Virgil's looking to score on one of your girls behind your back."

"No need to go behind my back. I said they're twins." He turned to Virgil. "You're taking me back to my car, aren't you?" Virgil nodded. "So come along up there with me and I'll introduce you. Turn on some charm and flex your muscles, and we'll see who gets which one. Not that I can ever tell 'em apart."

Landis came into the room from the direction of the men's quarters, his voice overriding Virgil's as Virgil started to answer. "No way! With an operation coming up in four days, we don't need a couple of guys who know all about it drinking their tongues loose in a bar somewhere, trying to impress women. I don't know about your outfit, Henkel, but my guys don't hang out in bars at a time like this. Virgil, you take our friend here out to his car and then turn your ATV around and come directly back. You understand?"

Elijah caught Virgil's look at Ham and Duane and then the wink he gave Henkel. "Yes, sir!" he answered. "Whatever you say, sir!"

"I mean it, Virgil!"

"Yes, sir!"

AlbanyNY: **timesunion.com: news**

TIMES UNION

Home: News: Today's Stories

by JAMES STURGIS, staff writer

First published: Monday, July 16, 2002

Explosion Kills Two

MALONE--In what authorities say appears to have been a terrorist plot gone awry, a bomb exploded in a car on the outskirts of the town of Malone yesterday evening.

Killed were two men, one tentatively identified as Bud Henkel, a member of the supremacist organization known as the White Nation. The other has yet to be identified.

It is thought that the two men were on their way to stage another of the bombings that have rocked the state in recent weeks.

"It could have been an accident with a timer," said a spokesman from the State Police. The severity of the explosion, which left the car demolished and a crater large enough to cause the closing of Highway 30, suggests that the intended target was a large one. "We don't know what they were after up here," the spokesman said, "but it looks like we lucked out this time."

Elijah pushed back from the computer, his stomach churning. Shakily he got to his feet and made his way out of the computer room, down the tunnel, up through the storage barn, and out. Then he began to run, skirting the edge of the lake. He ran past the cottage and into the woods, dodging rocks, leaping over roots and fallen trees, slipping on wet leaves. When he reached his boulder, he clambered onto it, ignoring the dampness of the rock seat. He pulled his knees up to his chin and sat, arms around his legs, eyes closed, trying to shut the newspaper story out of his mind.

I killed a man. Two men! The knowledge was like a splinter of ice in his heart. Some piece of him had known that the Wolf couldn't let a spy live. But he hadn't let himself think about that when he told what he'd learned. He had thought only of himself, of Amber and Cassie and the wolf pack. He had given no thought to the man with the rattlesnake tattoo, the man whose mind he had shared, who had loved coleslaw with barbecue. Dead now. And Virgil too. *If I hadn't told, they wouldn't be dead.*

If I hadn't told, he argued with himself, *the Wolf would be in jail now. Paradise Park shut down.* A memory floated back to him, a memory of two women pulling him from beneath a bush, taking him away in a car. *If I hadn't told, I'd be headed back to Children's Protective Services.*

A shadow passed over him, and a raven alighted on a nearby branch. It made no sound, only looked at him with its head cocked to one side. This was the first raven, he knew, the one that had come so long ago on the night he knew he was meant to live. The one that had stayed with him through the days in the den beneath the rocks when he'd almost died. It watched him now, unblinking. "So I'm still alive," he said, certain that it understood every word. "But those men are dead because of me. Both of them—dead. Gone forever."

The raven went on looking at him, and Elijah put his head down on his knees and closed his eyes, as if that way he could get away from the accusation he felt, from himself or from the bird, or both.

Quork.

As the sound faded on the air, Elijah felt himself slip out of his body like a balloon rising upward into a wide blue sky. Eyes open now, he could see ahead of him an eagle drifting on the wind. The bird tilted its wings, and Elijah found himself joined with it, sensing the wind's direction, feeling an insistent tug of hunger. He became aware of movement in a field of grass far below. A rabbit had hopped out of its burrow into the grass. The rabbit sat for a moment, ears twitching, and then began to eat.

The eagle angled its wings to make a sharp turn and began plummeting toward the ground, moving faster and faster as the grass seemed to rise to meet it. With a swoop, it struck at the rabbit with outstretched talons and angled upward again. The impact broke the rabbit's neck, and the eagle, pumping its wings against the added weight of the rabbit dangling limply from its talons, flew upward, a rush of satisfaction filling its body with the prospect of a meal.

Elijah felt himself slipping away from it, and then, as if in a film that had been rewound, he saw again what he had seen moments before—the eagle, talons empty, drifting on the wind. As it tilted its wings to circle above the grass, Elijah was pulled swiftly downward. He found himself joined with the rabbit then, looking out from a cup-shaped hole of trampled grass where it had been resting. Drawn by hunger and the scent of clover, the rabbit yawned, sniffed the air, and hopped out into the open, moving in the direction of the tantalizing smell. It hesitated, listening, and heard only the breeze in the tall grass. With a twitch of its nose it began to eat, nibbling the sweet white clover flowers.

Elijah, himself as well as rabbit, wanted to warn it of the eagle overhead, but his thoughts had no effect on the rabbit's awareness. From above came the sound of wind through feathers. Elijah tensed against what he knew was coming. There was a sharp blow, a flash of light, and then he felt himself, rabbit still, rising like smoke in the air.

There was no pain. No darkness. No closing down or ending, nothing he could feel as death. He seemed instead to be expanding, his consciousness joining with other rabbits that hopped, sniffed the air, nibbled grass or clover, even as he drifted in a sea of light. In a place of blue sky somehow separate from him the eagle flew on, the rabbit's body dangling from its talons. There was no connection now between that body and the sense of rabbit Elijah felt, still expanding.

Again it seemed as if the film had rewound. Again Elijah saw the eagle flying ahead of him, talons empty. The scene played out once more, Elijah joining this time with eagle and with rabbit, so that he felt himself to be three at once. He was eagle swooping, rabbit loosing itself from its body when struck, and himself, aware—himself in and around and through it all.

Then he was back again, sitting on his boulder, looking into the eyes of the raven. He sat very still, trying to sort through what had just happened, trying to understand.

It is not necessary to understand. The words formed clearly in his mind. *What you have experienced you know.*

Elijah played the scene over in his mind in all the

ways it had played out before. Himself as eagle, as rabbit, as both. He could relive what he had experienced, relive it again and again and again. But what was it he was supposed to know?

The sound of a raven's call echoed in the sky above them, and the raven cocked its head and lifted from the branch. Elijah watched it fly off between the trees, deftly moving upward as it went. It was going to join the others, he thought, going to join its family.

One thing Elijah did know. The wolf pack had become his family. He had acted to protect it. What else could he have done?

"Of course it was the right thing to do!" Amber dug her paddle into the water and angled the canoe away from the shore where a heron was fishing. In the bow seat Elijah moved his paddle slowly and stared into the green depths of the lake. He looked huddled into himself, his shoulders slumped, his legs tucked under the seat. She couldn't understand how he could doubt that telling Cassie had been right. However he felt about it, Amber was certain. The Henkel guy had *had* to die. "He would have destroyed us."

It chilled Amber to think of how easily everything her father had worked for, everything all of them had worked for, could come undone. One man. A man nobody had suspected till Elijah did that mind thing. Last night she'd had a dream—a nightmare—of men in uniforms surrounding Paradise Park, helicopters beating overhead, the sound of gunfire.

At lunch Kenny had said that they still didn't know if Elijah had been right about the man. "How could anybody prove it? There wasn't a single word about the FBI in the news," he pointed out. "Nothing about a government informant. All we know for sure is the guy's dead."

He had paused dramatically then. "And so is Virgil!"

As if the government would admit a thing like that, Amber thought, especially when the guy had been killed. The feds didn't tell the whole world about their failed missions.

"It isn't your fault about Virgil either," she told Elijah now. "He wasn't supposed to go with the guy. Dad says he disobeyed a direct order." Elijah didn't answer.

The heron stretched its neck and jabbed at the water with its pointed beak. Amber watched it bring up a wriggling fish and gulp it down, headfirst. "It's a war," she said. "And soldiers die in war. On both sides. They know that from the moment they join up."

Amber was having a difficult time feeling the way the others did about Virgil's death. He was one of the Cadre, a man she'd known most of her life, but it did no good to tell herself that. Something very strange had happened when she'd been reading the piece from the Albany paper about the deaths. They all had known by then that the unidentified man who'd died with the spy had to be Virgil. He had never come back from taking the man out to his car. So she was thinking about Virgil as she read, when she had a flash of memory: hands on her body in a dark tunnel. Those hands had been Virgil's. She didn't know how she knew it, but she knew it, as if the tunnel lights had come back on and she'd seen him. So certain was her knowing that it was hard for her, in that moment, to believe she hadn't known all along.

"Virgil disobeyed a direct order," she repeated. "And it got him killed. In the regular army if he'd disobeyed an officer in battle, the officer could have shot him for it. No difference."

The heron lifted itself from the water and flew across the lake in front of them. It didn't land in the shallows on the other side but rose into the air and skimmed away over the trees. Elijah watched it go, as intently as if he were seeing himself fly with it.

"Did you know about the spy before you got into his mind?" she asked him. "Did you know from the minute he came?"

Reluctantly, it seemed, Elijah drew his attention away from the sky where the heron had been just before it disappeared beyond the trees. He shook his head. "But all that day I had a feeling something bad was going to happen."

Amber remembered the way she'd felt that morning, as if she was coming down with stomach flu. And how she'd felt worse when she was with Elijah. She'd decided then that it was crazy to think there might be a connection. But she didn't know what was crazy anymore and what wasn't. Her feelings hadn't turned out to be stomach flu.

Maybe what they had been was her version of what Elijah had felt, her own premonition of something bad.

She looked at Elijah's back as he dug his paddle into the water. She could tell by the way he sat, the way he moved that he was still upset about the deaths. But more than that, she could feel it. She knew what her own feelings were. She was glad the spy had been killed before he could send the men with the uniforms. And she had felt nothing about Virgil since that memory of the hands, except a kind of vague relief. Those were her feelings, her own. Amber's. But beneath them she was aware of something else. A kind of dull, hollow, but insistent pain. Sadness. And a scattering of images like flashes of memory, memory that was not hers. An image of a fireball, something about coleslaw and barbecue.

Elijah had told her she was one of the Ark kids. She still didn't know what that meant for sure, but she was beginning to believe it.

part four

Biowar

MARCH

Kenny saw the dark shape in the snow and grinned. Finally! He'd been trying for months to get one of these birds, but they were too smart for snares and traps that could snag almost any other living thing. No matter how carefully he placed a bait and hid the snare, they noticed everything: tracks in the snow, even a difference in the texture of the snow when he'd carefully covered his tracks. But last night soft powder had fallen and covered everything with a light, even dusting, without completely obscuring the bait. Perfect. Mack was right. Patience, persistence, and determination eventually paid off.

When he got closer, his snowshoes sinking into the surface powder, he saw the single white feather on the raven's dark wing. This was the bird Kenny had seen with Elijah just yesterday. It had flown down to greet him when he left the lodge after breakfast heading for the computer center. It had landed in the snow on the porch railing and started chattering at the kid. Elijah, bundled in parka and scarf and boots, had stood and listened as if the bird was talking to him and he understood every word. Kenny had been watching through the window and, while the bird was still at it, had stepped out on the porch and slammed the door behind him. The raven, its single white feather catching the dawnlight, had flown off.

"Oh, jeez, did I scare it away? I'm *so* sorry!" Kenny had said, and then he'd gone back inside.

When the bird had flown, Elijah had looked at Kenny with that look he got sometimes that meant he was pissed but wasn't going to do anything about it. As if he could. Kenny had done something, though. That had been the last "conversation" this bird would have, with Elijah or anybody else.

Kenny took off his thick mittens and stuffed them into his parka pockets, then picked up the heavy bird, its eyes glazed in death, spots of blood frozen on its neck feathers, and loosened the wires that had strangled it. This wasn't one of the snares he'd found plans for on the nets; it was one he'd designed himself—tricky but deadly simple. He was excited about the way it had worked. Guns might be faster and more certain, but you had to be there when your target came within range. With a snare you could go on about your business and leave it to the animal to get itself killed. There was way more preparation, but way less waiting.

Kenny could hardly believe there had been a time

when he'd been afraid of Elijah's ravens, that first one and the others that had come later. As if Cassie's superstition could be right, as if killing one would bring some kind of vengeance down on all their heads. But there was nothing magic about them. He had the proof in his hands this minute. A dead bird. That's all it was. Big and heavy—and dead. Elijah's ravens might be smart, they might be harder than heck to catch, but they died just like anything else. No magic at all.

He stuffed the carcass into his backpack, blew on his fingers for a moment to warm them, his breath making clouds in the air, then slipped his hands back into his mittens. A few snowflakes drifted down from the thick gray clouds overhead. He would go over to the cottage when the coast was clear and leave a little surprise in Elijah's room, the room that had been Kenny's when they first came here, before he'd moved in with the soldiers where he belonged.

He had no fresh bait, so he put the snare into his pack as well. It wasn't likely that another raven could be caught in the same place as this one anyway. He'd have to start the whole process over again, leaving baits on the snow in a new place till the birds got used to finding them there and finally setting out the snare. He pulled his parka hood closer around his face as he walked. Maybe in time he could rid the place of all the ravens.

Maybe that would finally break the spell those birds had put first on Cassie and now on his father. They were always hanging around Elijah, chattering at him, making him seem like some kind of wizard or something.

The trouble was, it wasn't just the ravens that made everybody think that. Ever since Elijah had started talking, he had gone from a freak Charles Landis barely tolerated to some kind of genius who was going to do great things for the cause. Kenny's father had practically adopted the kid.

It made Kenny crazy. He was no dummy himself. As long as he could remember, he'd been able to do stuff *years* beyond what kids his age were doing in school. Nobody had ever made any big deal about it. Like it was just what was expected of the son of Charles Landis. Then Elijah starts talking, and Cassie pushes the kid so hard he manages to pass up Kenny, then Amber, and gets their father all googly-eyed about teaching him science. As if the Militia needed a scientist.

And what if the kid *was* a wizard with computers? When the Militia won the war, when it brought the system down, technology would be a thing of the past. Nobody would need computer techies then. What they'd need was somebody like Kenny: a good hunter, a good fighter, and smart enough to survive in whatever wilderness they'd have to deal with after civilization crashed.

Kenny had come out of the woods onto a long, rocky slope. The snow was falling harder now, and he picked up his pace, though his legs had started to ache from the snowshoe gait. As he walked, his head down against the rising wind, he thought back to September during one of his father's rarer and rarer visits to Paradise Park, when he'd asked to have Mack take over his education instead of Cassie. He'd planned his speech carefully beforehand. "Mack can teach me tactics and strategy and explosives and everything else I need to know. And the other guys have already been teaching me stuff like mechanics. The regular high school stuff I can get off the nets on my own."

His father had agreed so quickly it seemed as if he didn't care one way or another. As if Kenny's education didn't matter. What mattered was that Elijah was starting to take college courses on the nets. Like some freaking prodigy.

It had turned out okay, though, Kenny assured himself. Working with Mack was lots better than having to do whatever Cassie said. He was getting real experience now. Mack had let him have a part in the bombing of the microwave transmission towers when they finally pulled off the operation in October.

And ever since the feds raided the White Nation's compound, Mack had been setting up Paradise Park to withstand a siege, and he'd let him be part of that too, including the planning. His father might think Elijah was the next Einstein, but Mack understood that Kenny, thirteen years old now and almost as tall as Mack, was what the Militia really needed.

It had snowed enough that Kenny's outward-bound tracks had vanished already. He stopped for a moment, pulling out his compass to check his bearings before angling back into the woods. A dark shape materialized out of the snow, winging its way toward him from the trees ahead. A raven, flying low on the wind. It called loudly, once, twice, and Kenny ducked instinctively as it got close. Memory of his old nightmare came back to him. Nightmare, he told himself, firmly. Dream. Nothing real about it.

The bird went over his head, calling a third time. Kenny moved on. *Enjoy your life, bird,* he thought. *One of these days I'll be carrying you back in my pack.*

Quork.

Kenny looked up. Another raven was sitting on the bare branch of a tree a few feet away. As he went under it, it turned its head, following him with its eyes. Beneath his parka, he felt a chill on the back of his neck. A moment later both birds flew over him. One landed on an outcropping of rock and the other on a tree so that the way he was going he would have to walk between them. "Shoo!" he shouted at them, and waved his arms. They didn't move. He picked up a handful of snow, but it was too dry to pack. "Shoo!" he shouted again.

All right, he thought. *Don't shoo. I'll get you. Both of you. It's just a matter of time.*

The smell of damp soil and fertilizer and the warmth of the greenhouse wafted through the door and followed Elijah and Amber down the steps into the tunnel. Elijah hated the tunnels. No matter what the time of year, even in the spring when the blackflies swarmed, he would rather be out-of-doors than in the dim, chilly, damp gridwork of tunnels that now connected everything in the park. Whenever he had a choice, he moved from place to place on the surface. Even now, in the snow, he'd rather be up there, outside.

As if she'd picked up the thread of his thought, Amber said, "This is the kind of day I'm really glad we have the tunnels. I hate them in the summer, but in the winter . . ." She left the sentence dangling.

Elijah didn't answer. He loved the winter world, with its silence, the dark pattern of bare limbs against a white sky, the telltale footprints that reminded him of all the lives being lived beneath the snow. He liked the constant changes in the landscape as snow melted or piled up, the gray, blowing days and the sudden brilliant ones with the sun dazzling on the snow and the sky as deep blue as morning glories. But they had come from the cottage by tunnel that morning, wearing sweaters instead of parkas, so as the wind and snow raged above them now, they had to go back the same way.

"Cassie says the reason Dad's coming in tomorrow is to talk about the operation. Not *an* operation. *The.* As in *the biggest ever.*"

Walking behind Amber, Elijah grunted to let her know he was listening.

"She's been practically obsessed with the seed sprouting, as if this year we just *have* to raise enough over the summer to get us through next winter. It's only March, and we can't put most of the stuff outside till June, but look how many flats she's made us start already. I wonder what the operation is. If Cassie knows, she isn't telling. It doesn't make sense that any single operation can be *the* one. It goes against everything Mack says about guerrilla tactics."

Elijah had heard Mack say it often enough. "Like breaking stone. One small hit after another, over and over till the stone shatters." Elijah didn't like to think about big operations. The good thing about Mack's "small hits" was that people didn't die. The only person even seriously injured in one of them had been a man whose roof collapsed when a piece of a transmission tower fell on his house.

"There's something going on between Mack and Dad," Amber went on. "Have you noticed? Ever since the thing with the White Nation guy, Mack's been edgy when Dad's around. Like a cat with its fur up, you know? Just . . . edgy."

"Mmm."

"The thing is I don't know if we're ready for the big one. Oh, *we're* okay, I guess, but people outside—I don't know. The response to all the stuff we've put on the netsite about survival strategies and sustainability hasn't been that great lately. This time of year people don't want to think about vegetable gardens or food storage. They want to go skiing or skating or snowmobiling and then get back inside where it's warm. Watch TV. Mess around on the nets. There's just no way people want to think about how they're going to get along without technology, let alone make plans and really get ready. Not in the winter."

Amber turned down the tunnel that led around the lake to the cottage. Longer than any other, this tunnel was also narrower and lower, since it was used by so few people. She walked without speaking for a long time, and Elijah wondered what she was thinking. He had never purposely tried to join his mind with hers. Since the experience with Henkel, he had no wish to know more than anybody wanted him to know. But the connection between him and Amber wasn't something he could control. It was growing.

A few days ago she'd told him a nightmare she'd had, about a dark-skinned man beating a woman, then turning and coming after her. She had run outside, she'd told him, and crawled under some bushes. "I had a marble," she'd told him. "Like the one you had when you came here." Her nightmare had been his memory, his real life, but he hadn't told her that yet. The next night he'd had the dream about the red pickup truck. In it Kenny was a little kid in a car seat, crying, and the night was full of the sounds of guns. Even while he was dreaming it, he understood what it was. He knew now how Amber's mother had died. And what he'd recognized in her that very first night. He hadn't told Amber that yet either.

The day after the bombing of the microwave towers, when the news came out about the man who was injured, Amber had said the media were probably lying. Elijah, his mind starting to fill with images of fire and smoke, had made the mistake, then, of mentioning the Northway bombing, the deaths.

She had answered immediately, her voice firm. "Those were necessary losses." Elijah had felt her close down the instant he brought the subject up, so firmly that nothing came through to him except the sound of her words. She might have been a stone talking. It made him realize, suddenly, how much more he was used to picking up from people, even without trying, than the words they said. "We're in a war, Elijah. People die in war."

Now Amber had reached the stairway up to the cottage. "What I can't figure out is how one operation, no matter how big, could be the one that takes the whole system down. What Dad calls *the end of the world as we know it.*" She turned back to him, her foot on the first step. "Unless he's found some way to nuke Washington, D.C.!" Then she laughed and ran up the steps.

Elijah shivered as he followed her up.

"Okay, who's been out in the snow?" she asked from the living room of the cottage. He came up and lowered the trapdoor down over the stairs. Amber was standing with her hands on her hips, looking at the puddles where snow had been tracked through the hall by the front door, into the kitchen, and up the steps to the second floor. "It couldn't have been anybody from outside or the perimeter alarms would have sounded. Cassie's still in the greenhouse, and Dad doesn't come till tomorrow." She went out into the kitchen. "No mystery—it was Kenny. About half the cookies I made last night are gone."

Elijah stood looking at the wet tracks on the stairs. He felt a stir of apprehension as he started to follow them up. "Check my room," Amber called to him. "He probably built a snowman in the middle of my bed."

But the tracks didn't go to Amber's room. They led

directly to his own. He opened the door and saw the raven on his bed, its eyes glazed, its head wrenched to one side.

Elijah felt as if he'd been punched in the stomach. He stared at the single white feather on her wing. Yesterday this bird had come to him in the morning, her complex, liquid calls, xylophonelike bell sounds, and soft murmurings making the song of greeting and comfort she so often offered him. Kenny had come out and frightened her away, his only reason for coming onto the porch.

Rage washed over Elijah like a tidal wave. It was a good thing for Kenny that he'd left the bird and gone, Elijah thought. If he were here now, no matter how much bigger he was, how much stronger, Elijah would have taken him on and left him bloody. He kicked the leg of his bed and then slammed his fist into the wall, wishing it were Kenny's smirking face.

"What?" Amber called from downstairs. "What'd he do?"

Elijah didn't answer. Death, he had learned in dreamtime, was not end but transformation. It didn't help. He didn't want this bird transformed. Not this one! He didn't want her merging with all other ravens, flying and calling in another sort of world. He wanted her in this world, as this particular raven. His eyes blurring, he smashed the wall again.

When at last he was able to breathe evenly, he rubbed his raw knuckles and picked up the bird's stiff body. It meant nothing now. There was nothing of her left in it. He would take it to the woods, leave it on the snow where some hungry animal would find it.

As he started down the stairs, the thought struck him. Kenny had killed the raven, left its body in the cottage. That meant it no longer mattered to him what Cassie thought.

A table had been set on the raised platform at one end of the dining room in the lodge. Charles Landis sat there alone now, in his full dress uniform, complete with shiny black boots and red and gold epaulets on the shoulders of his tan uniform shirt. On the wall behind him was the banner of the Free Mountain Militia, with its outline of a mountain peak and the figure of a baying wolf. There was an open briefcase on the table in front of him. Amber sat between Cassie and Elijah with some of the men at one of the other two tables. There was a kind of excitement in the air that reminded her of the time at the old farm compound just before the Northway bombing. The expanded Cadre numbered fifteen now, and all of them had been called together after dinner for this meeting. Her father, with his "need to know" policy, had never before called a general meeting to talk about an operation before it had been completed, and Amber couldn't remember seeing him in uniform ever before except at public rallies.

He sat with his usual straight-backed posture, his jaw set, his face serious, but there was a kind of suppressed intensity radiating from him that everyone in the room seemed to be feeling and responding to. There was no doubt that Cassie was right. Whatever operation her father was going to tell them about, it was big. Amber glanced over at Kenny, who was sitting with Mack and the rest of the men at the other table. He was practically vibrating in his seat. Mack must have told him something about the importance of this operation too.

Charles Landis stood, cleared his throat, and the buzz of conversation stopped. He waited until the room was so quiet Amber could hear the wind in the trees outside. Then he walked around the table and began to speak, his voice not loud but clear and strong. "I'm aware that some of you have been critical of my choices lately. Apparently there is some thought that lobbying and political maneuvering aren't the best ways to accomplish our ultimate goal." His eyes scanned the room, resting on first one face, then another, some of the men fidgeting under his gaze. Mack, Amber noticed, had begun doodling on a legal pad on the table in front of him and did not meet his eyes.

"Well, you're absolutely right. Politics can't do what needs to be done." Mack looked up now. "What you don't know is why I've been doing it. I wasn't actually trying to change the system from the inside. What I wanted was the attention a high political profile brings. My goal was to attract others who share our beliefs, not just from America, but from the rest of the world as well."

There was a surprised murmur from the men. Amber glanced at Cassie to see if she had known this. Cassie's face was impassive, but she nodded her head almost imperceptibly.

Charles Landis began pacing as he talked, hand gestures emphasizing a word here, a phrase there. "As you all know, we have very little time. Environmental dominoes are falling faster than anyone predicted, and the world is teetering on the brink of disaster. The rich are growing ever richer, and the poor poorer, so violence continues to increase worldwide. Estimates used to give us until at least 2030 before current trends toward global disintegration would become irreversible. Those estimates have been revised. We have less than a decade. Political action is simply incapable of making change fast enough to save the earth."

Heads nodded around the room now.

"But neither can the methods of guerrilla warfare. We can't go on as we have. There just isn't time anymore for one small strike after another."

Mack frowned, set his pen down, and leaned forward, his elbows on the table.

"What we need is the capacity to cause sudden change on a global scale. Taking down a power station here, a computer or a telephone system there won't do it. We need a way to bring all of it down at once. Our own lives and the fate of the earth itself depend on it." Landis stood still then and looked from one face to another, making eye contact with each person in the room before continuing. When he looked at Amber, it felt as if he'd grabbed her, was holding her so that she couldn't look away.

"I've called you together tonight to tell you that I have a way to do that."

He raised his hands to quiet the stir that his announcement had made. "Three years ago I was contacted by a Russian scientist who came here shortly after the fall of the Soviet Union. He had been doing research there on biological warfare. When he came to America to work for a pharmaceutical firm, he brought everything he needed to continue his work under the cover of biomedical research. His beliefs coincide precisely with our own, and his goal is the same as ours. Together he and I have developed a plan. He provides the weapon; we take the action."

Amber had seen something about biological warfare on the nets. The weapons were germs. It had sounded like science fiction, and she hadn't paid much attention.

Her father went on, his voice growing gradually more intense. "The operation we've planned is simple, elegant, and irreversible. Once it begins, there will be no way to stop it or even appreciably slow its effects. In less than a year it will bring about the total collapse of technological civilization, not just here but all over the world. And it will take a handful of men less than a single day to accomplish it."

Murmurs of disbelief ran through the room. Landis smiled, the lines around his eyes deepening, and waited till the men were quiet again. Then he looked at Cassie. "You'll appreciate the irony of Yvgeny's particular weapon, Cassie. Our government has used this weapon before—against your people. You remember the infected blankets?"

Cassie, sitting next to Amber, stiffened in her chair. "You don't mean smallpox?"

Landis nodded. "I do. It's contagious, and it's lethal. More important, modern medicine was supposed to have eradicated it. Smallpox vaccinations were discontinued in the last quarter of the twentieth century because the vaccine had become a greater risk to the public health than the disease itself. Those people still around who were vaccinated as children are no longer protected. The vaccine has worn off. If smallpox is introduced to the world's population now, it will spread the way it spread among the Indians who had never been exposed."

The room was absolutely quiet. Amber's hands had gone cold. All along she had been aware of Elijah on her left, Cassie on her right. But now it was as if they had disappeared. Elijah, Cassie, Kenny, all the men. There was only her father and the silence after his words.

Mack spoke then. "That means none of *us* is immune."

Landis moved back to the table and took a glass vial filled with clear liquid from his open briefcase. "Not yet." He held the vial up. "My Russian friend has provided the virus, engineered to be even more deadly than the original, and also the vaccine that he developed from the new virus."

Ham LaFontaine cleared his throat.

"You have a question?"

"I don't see how this does what we want to do. We want to destroy the system, not the human species."

Amber's mind seemed to have gone numb. What did Ham mean? Her father wasn't talking about destroying the human species!

Landis smiled broadly. "That's the beauty of this plan. No disease kills everyone. It's the earth's own defense mechanism. Even without the vaccine, there will be people with some degree of natural immunity. They may catch it, but they won't die of it. Smallpox in its natural form killed about a third of the people who contracted it, and even this new strain is unlikely to be lethal to more than half. That's enough to destroy the system, virtually overnight, but there will be enough survivors to continue the species on a more moderate scale. Cassie—"

Amber looked at Cassie, whose face seemed almost drained of color.

"When you sow seeds, Cassie, and they start coming up, you have to thin them, don't you?"

Cassie nodded.

"Because if you left them all to grow, they would compete with one another for nutrients and sunlight. The whole crop would be stunted. Worst-case scenario, overcrowding could lead to the loss of the whole crop. What we're going to arrange here is a global thinning. The species will be the better for it eventually. In the meantime the earth will be saved from human technology. Best of all, because only humans get smallpox, all the other living species will be unharmed."

Amber's mind jolted sideways. She had read about a scientist who wanted to create a bomb that would wipe out all life forms but leave buildings and roads and electrical systems—all of human technology—intact. The bomb had never been made. Too terrible, people said. Too terrible even to think about. Why had she thought of that? What her father was talking about was different. Different. Almost the opposite!

"How does it get to be global?" one of the men

asked. "If we release smallpox somewhere near here, what makes you think it'll spread that far?"

"Another little irony," Landis said. "Next month the third international convention on counterterrorism is being held in Albany. Delegates from nearly every country in the world will attend. They will meet in one building, to which we have access. We release the virus into the ventilation system, and when the conference is over, the delegates return to their own countries, unknowingly carrying smallpox with them. Meantime, of course, they circulate among their fellow airplane passengers, the people they come into contact with in airports, taxis, buses. Their families. Their friends. Until people begin to show symptoms, which takes days, no one will know it happened. When the first symptoms appear, few doctors will recognize them. They won't have seen a case of smallpox. Not till the blisters appear will it be recognized. Unlike a bomb, which brings the authorities immediately, this weapon alerts no one."

Elijah had drawn his feet up onto his chair, was sitting now with his arms clasped around his legs, head down on his knees, eyes tightly closed.

"So how do we know the vaccine works?" Mack asked.

"It's been thoroughly tested."

"Is it dangerous?" Duane asked.

"Good question." Landis held up the vaccine again. "In the tests this stuff had no serious side effects. But no vaccine is one hundred percent safe. That's why they quit vaccinating people when smallpox disappeared from the general population. Yvgeny tells me that no one on whom this vaccine has been tested has had anything more than a little inflammation and a brief fever."

"So we get a shot," Ham said, "and when everybody else gets sick, we're okay. Who else gets the vaccine?"

"I have enough for the rest of the Militia and their families and for some of the allies Mack has been working with."

"Isn't it a considerable security risk to give that many people the vaccine and alert them ahead of time to what we're doing?" Mack asked.

"Not if we tell them it's a high-dose vitamin shot."

It wasn't only her hands that were cold now, Amber realized. She looked around, half expecting to see a window open, letting in the freezing March night.

Elijah woke from a nightmare and burrowed under his blankets. He couldn't remember anything about the dream except the horror, which came into waking with him. But he was sure it had been about smallpox. In the morning everyone was to get a vaccination. Landis himself was going to do the injections.

For a long time Elijah lay in a cocoon of warmth that did nothing to warm him. "Necessary losses," Amber had said of the people who died in the Northway bombing. It was what her father had taught her. If the Wolf was right about what he meant to do, half of all the people on the earth would be the necessary losses this time. And the other half—Elijah couldn't imagine how it would be for the other half. It would be better to be one of those who died than one of those who were left, he thought, with people dying all around you.

The population of the United States was almost 280 million people. Half that: 140 million. It was an impossible number, one so big he couldn't get a sense of it. He'd seen a picture on the nets of a demonstration in Washington, D.C., where people had been jammed together as far as you could see into the distance so that the ones in the back didn't look like people anymore, just tiny blotches of color. But that crowd, like an ocean of people, had been only thousands. One hundred forty million people were thousands of times that many. If Landis did what he was planning, that many people would be dead. One hundred forty million bodies. What could be done with 140 million bodies? And that would be only in America! It didn't count the billions of people in the rest of the world.

Half the people of the world. Half the doctors would die, and half of all the other people who worked at hospitals, half the police and half the military and half the leaders who'd be trying to handle the catastrophe. How many orphans would there be, and who would look after them? And how many people who didn't actually die would get sick? Who would take care of the sick ones?

Elijah could scarcely believe a person—any person—could consider doing such a thing. But people *had* been considering it. Planning it. Working on ways to do it. Not just the Wolf and the Russian scientist. Whole governments. There were countries, Charles Landis had said, that had stockpiles of missiles already loaded with bioweapons—not smallpox but germs almost as bad. Some of those weapons had been used already. In a world of people who made war, this was just business as usual.

He thought of what the Ark kids had wanted to do, what they'd almost managed, joining their minds together to tame the violence in other people. Impossible, he saw now. It didn't matter how many Ark kids there were or how many individual violent acts they could manage to keep from happening. Violence wasn't about individual acts. Even individual humans. It was underneath everything, a violence more horrible than anything he'd ever imagined. It was there in the way human beings were made. The job was too big.

"Everybody knows that eventually someone will unleash a biological weapon in a major population center," the Wolf had said. "The only question is who, and when, and how well. Better us now than someone else later, when we won't have a vaccine to be sure we survive. It's us or them. I say let it be us."

And the others had agreed.

Elijah had sat stunned, clutching his knees. He had seen it. *The others had agreed.* Cassie, Ham, the O'Donnells. Mack had asked a lot of questions. But he hadn't protested, hadn't refused to go along with it. His problems with the idea had nothing to do with how many people would die or how they would die or what the world would be like for the survivors. They were about technicalities. Safety. Whether they could be sure it would work. By the end of the meeting the Cadre had been ready to do what Landis said. As always. It was the ideal solution, the alpha wolf had assured his pack, a weapon that used nature's own methods against the species that was destroying nature.

Worst of all had been Amber's reaction. Elijah had felt nothing from her. No horror, no disgust or even fear. She had sat very still listening to her father, and he had felt nothing from her at all.

Elijah tried to go back to sleep, but he couldn't. His mind was full of images, one more terrible than the next. It was like a nightmare he couldn't wake up from. Finally he got out of bed and wrapped a blanket around him. Moonlight, reflected off the snow of the porch roof, filled his room with a soft bluish light. He padded across the cold wood floor to the old wooden rocking chair he had set next to the window. The silence of the winter night outside was almost tangible.

There were life-and-death struggles going on out there in that silence, he thought—owls flying soundlessly among bare trees, watching for the movement of mice and voles that dared venture out of their tunnels beneath the snow to forage for grass seeds. Bobcats hunting rabbits. All part of what Cassie called the web of life. Had human beings ever just fitted into that web, or had they always insisted on trying to control it, choosing which parts would stay and which parts would disappear forever?

Elijah sat in the chair, his legs crossed under him, his blanket clutched around him. He thought of the Ark family. Where were they tonight? What were they doing? It had been three years. Doug and Miranda were too old by now to be at Laurel Mountain still. Taryn had nowhere else to go. When the smallpox was released, they wouldn't be protected by the vaccine. Which of them would die?

Cassie in flannel pajamas and a heavy robe sat at the conference table in the War Room, her hair unbound, its blue-black sheen spilling over her shoulders, her arms folded across her chest. Charles Landis, his tie loosened, his uniform shirt open at the throat, paced the room like a tiger testing the limits of its cage.

"I don't think you appreciate how much effort I've put into making this all happen. Yvgeny had already engineered the new virus when he contacted me. But it's taken three years to get to the point where we can use it. Three years of frustration—negotiating the price, waiting for Yvgeny to finish the testing, getting thrown back to square one over and over again when vaccine after vaccine failed."

He gestured toward the black leather case that stood open on the end of the table. Inside, the right half of the case was divided into square compartments of gray foam rubber, each containing a glass vial. The undivided half was full of disposable syringes, each in its own plastic envelope. "This is the most valuable stuff in the world." Landis ran a hand through his white hair. "You wouldn't believe the difficulties we ran into. Lab mice had to be genetically engineered so they could contract the new strain of smallpox. Then Yvgeny would try a vaccine. And as many vaccinated mice would die as unprotected ones. Then he'd try another. And another. And another. I almost gave it up. Everything obviously depends on the certainty that our people will be absolutely protected."

"Obviously," Cassie said.

"Then a batch of vaccine turned out to be even more deadly than the disease itself. Every other time the mice had been vaccinated, they'd been perfectly okay till they were exposed to the virus. This time, within a few hours after they were injected with the vaccine, they started to die. And not just a few! Every single one of them. Yvgeny said it was a weapon in itself, that vaccine. I almost canceled the whole project then and there.

"But he convinced me to wait for one more round of experiments. He said he was closer than ever. The problem with the deadly vaccine was the key to producing one that would work. I can hear him now, with that cartoon character Russian accent of his: 'It will take only a small genetic—how you say?—*twiddle* to fix.'

"Turned out he was right. The next vaccine worked. All the mice stayed healthy from the moment they were vaccinated, right through their exposure to the virus, till they were killed and dissected to be sure that there was no sign of virus, no sign of damage. Then he tried it on people, prisoners who thought it was research for a new flu vaccine. It worked there too. With not a single serious side effect."

Charles Landis leaned against the table near Cassie. His face was flushed; his eyes gleamed. "You wouldn't believe how simple this whole thing is going to be. I did the dry run myself. I put a little coconut oil into the ventilating system of the conference center where the antiterrorism conference is going to be held. It spread through the building exactly the way the virus will spread. The whole dispersal took no more than a matter of minutes. Over the next hour I went into every room in the building, and the coconut scent was detectable in every single one. Everywhere the scent of coconut reached, the virus will reach. The people who come to the conference will turn into human missiles, carrying our weapon back to their home countries. And no one will suspect a thing. Simple. Elegant. Perfect."

Cassie sat for a moment, as still as if she were carved from stone. Then she shook her head. She pushed herself to her feet, still shaking her head, and went to the door. She turned back, her hand on the doorknob. "No." There were tears in her eyes. Almost angrily she brushed them away. "I have loved you more than my life. But if you do this, you will do it without me. When they used smallpox against my people, it was genocide. Ignorant white men who believed that the only good Indian was a dead Indian. What you're planning to do is something else. It isn't one race, one people against another. It's humanity eating itself up. I don't have to forgive what was done to us to know it must never be done again."

With that she opened the door and went out, closing it firmly behind her.

Elijah stared out into the night, rocking slightly. There was no escaping the images of death. Everything came back to that. He closed his eyes, willing himself away from his own mind, away from the images, the feelings of terror and grief they brought with them. And felt the sinking sensation that signaled the joining of consciousness.

He felt as if he'd been thrown into a whirlpool, sucked downward into movement and darkness and cold. Then he was looking out from another set of eyes. What he saw through those eyes was the inside of the War Room, its maps on the wall, tacks in place to mark completed operations.

Layer after layer of thought and memory and feeling welled up, competing for his attention. Elijah tried to maintain his image of himself, Elijah, separate and distinct, like a passenger in this body, its eyes like windows he could peer out of. But he could not. Feelings buffeted him, surging around and through—anxiety, anger, and something deep and painful that slipped into place inside him as if Elijah had known it all his life. Inexorably, as if a lifeline were slipping through his hands, he lost contact with his sense of self and shifted into the other. He felt his hands, one with a wolf tattoo, clenching and unclenching, felt a pulsing throb in his temple.

No. Absolutely not! The thoughts were like cannons going off in Charles's head. He refused to accept the possibility that now, with the goal so close, Cassie would pull back. She had pledged her life to him and to their work. She wouldn't, she couldn't walk away from that pledge. The government had taken Marion away from him. Marion and Terrence both—the most important people in his world. He would not allow another loss.

He looked at his watch. It was nearly three in the morning, and Cassie hadn't slept yet. What she needed was rest, a little sleep to let the idea sink in, settle into her mind, as it eventually had to do, it was so perfect. This was just an emotional overreaction. A little sleep, that was all. She'd come around.

He could use some sleep too, he thought. But not yet. There was something he needed to decide about first, something more important than Cassie's little tantrum. Mack.

The thought of Mack's reaction to his plan sent his heart racing with fury, his blood pounding in his temple. Mack had asked question after question. The questions weren't the problem. They were proof that he was thinking, measuring, evaluating the weapon and the dispersal system, exactly as he should, since he would command the men who carried out the operation. The problem was in his eyes—his eyes and his body language. Charles Landis hadn't gotten where he was without being able to read more than a person's words.

What he had read in Mack this evening was all wrong. Never once had he met Charles's eyes. Instead he had watched the other men, and Charles had seen how he was gauging their reactions. Calculating. Twice he had seen Mack and Ham LaFontaine lock eyes and exchange—what?—the twitch of an eyelid, the smallest distension of a nostril. The two of them had been humoring him. Their agreement with the plan had been a lie, a show. They had not, like the others, been swayed by the perfection of it, the delicious irony of releasing the ultimate bioterrorist weapon at the international antiterrorist conference.

Cassie had warned him that he was away from Paradise Park too much, had turned over too much authority to Mack. The men were developing a strong loyalty to Mack, she'd told him more than once. Maybe too strong. But he'd been caught up in the problems of the vaccine; there had been too much else to do, too much else to think about.

He looked at the maps on the walls, their pins representing a power plant here, a transmission tower there. Mack's kind of war. Smallpox was another kind, a war that needed none of Mack's expertise—no explosives, no precise military planning, no advances and retreats. He had thought Mack cared about the mission, the goal, more than his methods, more than his own power and control. He had been wrong.

Mack wouldn't betray him to the authorities. He had too much to lose himself. Not betrayal. Mutiny. Mack would turn the men against him, take control of the Cadre, then the Militia.

Charles threw himself down on a chair and sat, tapping the conference table with his fingers, the wolf tattoo rippling as the tendons moved under the skin of his hand. He had needed Mack, trusted and respected him. No one else could have pulled off the bombings so cleanly, with no loose ends except those that would lead the authorities in other directions, to the White Nation and the Canadian militias. No one else could have overseen the finishing of this compound, this bunker they could live in until the repercussions of the smallpox devastation had spun themselves out. But now everything that had made Mack the perfect second-in-command, the perfect beta wolf, was about to backfire.

The beta wolf was going to mount a challenge. Charles didn't know how. He only understood that it would happen. And soon.

He made a fist, watching the skin smooth and the outlines of the wolf tattoo grow taut. Marion and Terrence

HIGH FRONTIER
SCHOOL LIBRARY

were gone. The hole their murders had left in his life had never been filled. Not by Cassie, much as he depended on her, and certainly not by Mack. He had trusted the man, and he'd been wrong. But he knew what to do about it.

He would strike before Mack had a chance to act. If one of them was going to lose, it would be the beta, not the alpha wolf. Not the alpha wolf! It needed to be quick and undetectable. If the men thought he had struck Mack down, there was no way to be certain they wouldn't turn on him. So far he had played it carefully, giving no hint of his own suspicions. Mack had no reason to think Charles was aware of his own danger.

He pulled the black case across the table to him. Under the syringes in the corner opposite the vials of vaccine was a small black plastic box. He took it out and opened it. Inside was a vial, like the others except for the small red dot affixed to its label. He had slipped it into his pocket during one of his visits to Yvgeny's laboratory. "A weapon in itself" Yvgeny had called the deadly batch of vaccine, and Charles had understood immediately that it could be useful. Yvgeny had understood the same thing; he had not destroyed the faulty batch, merely marked each vial and stored it in its own section of the freezer.

The vaccine was to be administered tomorrow. Charles felt the feelings that had raged inside him all night settle into a calm, cold stillness. It was simple, really. He would begin with Mack. Charles removed the first vial in the first row of compartments and replaced it with the one with the red dot. Then he took it out again and peeled the dot off the label. There must be no difference between this bottle and the others. They must look the same.

He wouldn't have to worry about making a mistake, even with the telltale dot missing. Location was the key. The deadly vaccine was the first one in the first row, easy enough to remember.

Calmly Charles Landis closed the case and latched it. He hated losing Mack. He was the best man the Militia had ever had. They would need all the manpower they could muster to keep Paradise Park running and defend it from other survivors once the system had disintegrated under the onslaught of the new plague. But it could not be helped.

Paradise Park. Landis smiled. The world was full of ironies. Because some fool had chosen that grandiose name for his summer camp nearly a century ago, the seeds of the earth's next civilization would be sown in Paradise. His smile faded.

It was not Cassie he wanted to share his triumph with; it was Marion. She should have been here tonight. Terrence too. The catastrophe he was about to unleash on the world was not enough to make up for their loss. But the new civilization that would be established when it was over, a civilization that would exist in rhythm with the earth, would be a fitting tribute.

Elijah was lost in the dark, overwhelmed with grief and fury. Mama Effie was dead. His mother was dead. He had been left alone in the world by a man who had beaten him, killed his mother, a man who cared nothing for anyone or anything except himself. The Man deserved to die. Wherever he was in the world now, in prison or on the streets somewhere, the Man deserved to die. Let him pay for what he'd done. Let smallpox take him down.

Elijah understood more clearly than he ever had before how terrible a place the world was. A hostile and dangerous place. It was full of stupid people, vicious, shortsighted people who put themselves first, who acted out their fantasies, their wishes, with no regard for others. No regard for the planet or the future. The Ark family hadn't understood their quest, but he could see now what it was. He was here in this place, with these people, because he was an alpha cub learning from the alpha wolf.

Memories of news stories he had read on the nets came back to him, stories of war and murder and destruction. In a world of violence, of guns and bombs and fires, a planet that was being raped and murdered by a culture of human technology, he had a purpose, and he saw clearly now what that purpose was. Doug had been right. To save the world, you had to take out the people who would destroy it.

What did losses matter in such a world? They were necessary losses. What were the lives of individual humans against the life of the planet? Necessary losses!

Elijah.

The virus was a small thing, as he had been small when the Man came into his life, bringing the growl, the roar of his violence. Yet this small thing would take over the world. It would be the revenge of the small against the huge and powerful. He had run before, had spent his life running, but he would never, never run again.

Elijah.

His name. The sound echoed in his mind and began to pull him away from the enveloping darkness. He didn't want to go. This was where he belonged, where his part of the quest had brought him. The darkness sucked at him as something else struggled to pull him free. He felt he would be torn apart, as wolves tear apart the body of an animal they have brought down. Wolves. The Wolf.

The image of a hand filled his mind, a hand with a wolf tattoo. It was not his own hand.

He opened his eyes. He was in the rocking chair in his

room, his blanket bunched on the floor, his body chilled through. He reached down and pulled the blanket up around him.

He sat shivering, staring out his window into the snowy world where the first light of dawn was softening shadows, until warmth returned and his body settled. He had merged with Charles Landis and, in the merging, had lost himself. Except that it had not felt like loss. It had felt like recognition. There was nothing in Charles Landis that Elijah could not find in himself. They were one. As he had been one with bear and raccoon, eagle and rabbit. But if that was so, what had called him back from Landis, pulled him free of the dark swirl of his own grief and fear and hatred, his own wish for revenge? What had brought him back into his body?

He closed his eyes, exhausted suddenly, and took a long, slow breath. He became aware of Amber, dreaming above him, Cassie, tossing in an uneasy doze across the hall. Fine threads of connection reached out to him, bound him into the silent cottage. What he wanted now was to sleep. He stood, gathering the blanket around him, and crept across the cold floor to his bed. As he slipped toward sleep, a raven lifted into the air outside the window and disappeared into the gradually lightening sky.

The three of them, Cassie, Amber, and Elijah, had eaten breakfast at the cottage. Amber had no memory of it. She had, in fact, little memory of anything since the meeting last night and even less of the meeting itself. Her father in his dress uniform, the Militia banner on the wall behind him—those images were all she could call up. But they were as clear as the memory of the first time she had seen her father in that uniform standing on a platform in front of a crowd of people speaking into a microphone. The sun had been full and bright that day and had shone straight down on him, glinting off his white hair and the gold epaulets on his shoulders, making a kind of glow around him. Amber remembered thinking it could have been an angel in that glow instead of her father, until he spoke, his voice so clear and loud and unmistakable.

She had been standing in the crowd, her hand held firmly by the woman her father had hired to watch over her and Kenny. A woman, she remembered, with dark hair and a reddish purple stain across half her face, who had frightened Kenny to tears the first time she came to the basement apartment they were living in at the time.

But Kenny had grown used to the woman, who had never punished him for the names—Scarface and Grape Jelly and Splotchy—he called her. "Whatever you think up to call me," she'd said, "I've been called worse."

Amber wondered why she could remember that woman, who'd been fired for snooping and disappeared from her life when Amber was no more than eight years old, when she couldn't remember what her father had said only a few hours ago. She knew it had been about the operation, a perfect plan that would do what the Militia had been working to do from the very beginning. But the details of the plan had faded, like the nightmare that had wakened her this morning and then vanished, leaving only a trace of feeling, like a toothache, that she couldn't shake.

As they walked the dim tunnel to the lodge, where another meeting was to be held, Amber assured herself that everything would come back to her as soon as her father started speaking. It had to have been the impact of the forgotten nightmare that had shaken her enough to drive everything else from her mind. She followed Cassie's hunched shoulders, aware of Elijah's footsteps behind her. No one spoke as they walked.

When they came up into the dining room of the lodge, the men were milling around among the newly cleared tables, talking in low tones, some of them still holding their coffee mugs. The O'Donnells were cleaning up in the kitchen. Kenny sat at a table with Mack, pushing his own mug back and forth between his hands. Speaking to no one, Cassie sat down at an empty table. Amber sat next to Cassie, Elijah next to Amber. There was a table on the raised platform, and Amber remembered that it had been there last night, under the Militia banner, her father leaning against it as he spoke. He was not there now. Chilled from their walk through the tunnel, Amber sat hunched in her chair, her hands in her armpits to warm them.

Elijah sat next to Amber, fighting off despair. He had had another nightmare in the little sleep he had managed since dawn. He remembered no more of it than he remembered of the first, except a lingering sense of horror.

When Charles Landis came up from the War Room, carrying the black case, the dining room fell silent. He set the case on the front of the platform, and the men who were not yet seated found places at the tables. Elijah stared at the case, wishing he could rush up, smash it to the floor, and stomp on it until all the vials were destroyed, the vaccine nothing but a spreading puddle. It would not help, of course. The Wolf would only go back to the scientist and get more vaccine. More of both kinds. Smashing the case would only delay the vaccinations—and probably get Elijah killed. Landis was willing to kill Mack, his oldest ally, on a whiff of suspicion. He would kill Elijah with no more thought than squashing an ant.

Elijah felt the tension in the air. What, he wondered, had the men been talking about before Landis came in? Had any of them had nightmares during the night? Were any of them having second thoughts?

Kenny, who'd been sitting at Mack's table, went to join his father at the platform. "Can I help?" he asked.

"Get some cotton balls, some small Band-Aids, and a bottle of alcohol from the first-aid kit in the kitchen."

While Kenny went to do as he was told, Elijah tried to sense what Amber was feeling. But there was nothing. It was as if she had surrounded herself with armor, invisible but impenetrable.

Suddenly an image from his nightmare flashed through his mind. He and Amber were standing together at the edge of a deep ravine as a bulldozer pushed a mountain of bodies, covered with dark red blisters, over the edge. Had they shared the nightmare? He glanced at her. Frowning, she ran a hand through her hair. The armor was cracking, he realized. She *had* had the nightmare. It had been her memory of it just now that awakened his own.

On the other side of Amber Cassie sat, her hands folded in front of her, her face impassive. She would do nothing to interfere with the vaccinations, Elijah thought. What she might do afterward, Elijah didn't know. He supposed it was possible that Charles Landis had been right. She had pledged her life not just to him but to his mission. It was possible he could win her back.

It occurred to him then that everyone here was as helpless in the face of the Wolf's plan as he was, at least for now. He glanced around the room at the tight, tense faces. He had thought they had all agreed to it before. But now he wasn't so sure. Some of them could be feeling as he did, as Cassie felt, as Amber did too, no matter how hard she tried to close the feelings off. And what of Mack? From where Elijah sat, he couldn't see the man's face. Could Mack begin a mutiny here, now? Were enough of the men on his side? Could a wolf pack ever just refuse to go along with the alpha wolf?

Kenny brought the alcohol, Band-Aids, and cotton balls, and Charles Landis opened the case.

Landis took a stack of syringes from the case and set them on the platform next to it, then pulled a pair of reading glasses out of the pocket of his shirt and put them on. "Elijah," he said, "get a trash can, would you? Kenny, you soak a cotton ball in alcohol and swab each person's arm as he comes up. I'll give the shot. Then you put on a Band-Aid. The trash goes in the can, and we're on to the next person."

Elijah, his mind racing to come up with something he could do to stop what was coming, went to the kitchen for a trash can. He carried it out and set it on the floor by Kenny and moved to the other side of Charles Landis. Some of the men were fidgeting in their seats. "Mack," Landis said, "it looks like some of the guys aren't crazy about needles. Why don't you go first, show them there's nothing to be afraid of?"

The bad vaccine was in the first vial in the bottom row, Elijah knew, with nothing to mark it clearly different from the others. *First vial in the top row!* Elijah sent the thought with every ounce of mental energy he could muster. He'd done it before, sending math principles to Amber. Maybe he could confuse Landis into taking a different vial. *Top row!* Landis blinked, looked into the case, and frowned. *First vial in the top row!* Elijah thought again. What good was a new kind of mind if it couldn't do this?

Landis ran a hand over his mouth and gave his head a little shake. Then he withdrew the first vial in the bottom row. The vial with the deadly vaccine.

Duane Bruder was waving a hand. "I don't know about this! I had a buddy in the army had to get vaccinated against anthrax. A bunch of soldiers got sick—really, really sick—from the vaccinations. My buddy's been on disability for ten years because of it. How do we know that isn't going to happen here?"

Landis shook his head. "Because I told you so. The vaccine has been tested. The only side effects were some redness and a little fever."

Some of the other men began murmuring to one another. Now that Duane had made the first objection, others began to talk about stories they'd heard about the vaccines the military used to protect against biological weapons. Landis let them go on for a time and then set the vaccine down next to the case and held up both hands for silence. "All right, all right. I understand your concern. You don't know the scientist who made this vaccine. I'm the one who knows him, I'm the one who's been working with him for three years to develop this plan. And I trust him and his experiments completely. Will you feel better if I give *myself* the first shot?"

Elijah felt a tremor run through his body. Maybe there was a way to stop the operation after all.

Landis had turned back to the black case and was picking up one of the plastic-wrapped hypodermics from the pile next to it. As he did so, he pushed the first vial of vaccine under the needles. He rolled up the sleeve of his shirt, exposing the skin of his upper arm.

Elijah needed a distraction of some kind. Something big. Something that would take everyone's attention somewhere else. Away from this end of the room. He could think of nothing. *Help!* he thought, unsure whom he was calling to.

Landis was playing the moment for effect, holding up the plastic wrapper so that everyone could see him tear it open and remove the needle.

Help! Elijah thought again, and the image of a raven came to him. Raven challenging wolf.

As Landis reached toward the case, toward the vial in the second compartment, there was a resounding crash at the front of the lodge, followed by the sound of glass breaking. The window next to the front door shattered inward, and a black bird crashed to the floor in a cascade of broken glass.

It took Elijah no more than a moment to recover from the shock. He moved like lightning, snatching the first vial from beneath the pile of syringes and switching it with the one Landis had been reaching for. The whole thing took no more than a few seconds, as Landis and everyone else moved automatically toward the mess by the window. Cold air swept into the room, and Mack sent one of the men to get plastic and tape to cover the window and another for a broom.

"I thought those birds were supposed to be so smart," Kenny said. "That's got to be the stupidest thing I've ever seen."

Cassie knelt gingerly on the glass-littered floor and reached a hand toward the bird. "It's dead."

"Duh!" Kenny said.

Only then did Elijah allow himself to look.

It was the first raven. He recognized it with a certainty that seemed to lodge his heart in his throat, closing it off so that he could neither swallow nor take a breath.

Cassie lifted the bird gently, cradling its drooping head. "Broken neck," she said.

Numbly, Elijah moved toward her. She held the body out to him. He took it and carried it outside. He barely felt the cold as he walked down the steps of the lodge porch and into the woods. The wind ruffled black feathers, and Elijah blinked back tears that threatened to freeze on his eyelashes. *I didn't mean for you to do this,* Elijah thought as he laid the bird on the snow beneath a cluster of birch trees. But as he thought it, he understood that the raven had done what had to be done, as Elijah had. He stroked the smooth feathers, thinking of a drift of light, of smoke on the wind. *Fly safely.*

He hurried, then, back to the lodge. What the raven had done was over. What *he* had done was just beginning. It was something, he knew, that would be with him for the rest of his life.

When he went inside, stomping snow from his feet, the mess had been swept away, the window covered. Landis was filling a syringe with the vaccine from the second compartment, the vial Elijah had switched, the vaccine that had killed all the mice. Quickly, cleanly, Landis gave himself the injection. Kenny put the Band-Aid in place, and then Landis turned to the men. "Just in case that doesn't set your minds at rest, I'll do family next. Amber. Then Kenny. Then Cassie."

He motioned Amber forward. She came, pushing up the sleeve of her sweater. Landis opened another hypodermic and began to fill the second syringe. Elijah felt ice water flow through his veins. Landis was using the same vial of vaccine. Each one must contain enough for two doses. *No! No!* But it was too late. Already he was injecting the vaccine into Amber's arm. While Kenny put the Band-Aid on his sister's arm, Landis dropped the empty vial into the trash. He would never know what he had done.

But Elijah knew. He ran into the bathroom and vomited his breakfast.

Later that morning Charles Landis spiked a fever. By afternoon Amber was complaining of a headache; when Cassie took her temperature, it was 103. By evening both were in bed in the cottage with fevers hovering near 105, ugly blotches of red spreading over their necks. Their faces grew puffy, their eyes swollen shut. Cassie, tending to both of them, sent Elijah to use his hands to work on Landis as she sponged Amber with alcohol to bring her fever down.

Elijah stood for a long time at Landis's bedside, looking down at the man whose consciousness he had shared, whose grief and rage and sense of betrayal had been his own. Landis tossed and moaned, eyelids puffed closed over the icy blue eyes. The hand with the wolf tattoo moved restlessly on the damp sheet, fingers swollen, the outline of the wolf's head black against red skin. That hand had been his own hand, Elijah thought. His own fist, clenching and unclenching.

He knew something now that he didn't think the Ark family had understood, something maybe no one could understand using the part of the mind called intelligence, the part that had seemed to make the Ark kids so different from others, the part that had brought them together in the first place. When Taryn taught them to reach their minds out to the consciousness of trees, clouds, animals, mountains, she had thought she was teaching them how to make a connection, one separate mind to another.

But there was no need to reach. They had only to *shift*. The connection was there all along because they were not separate—tree, cloud, animal, mountain, human. Different but not separate. Consciousness, Elijah knew now, was one thing, that thing Cassie called the web of life. It was a single pattern that all belonged to, all were part of, connected and intertwined. If it was true that the Ark kids brought something new into the world, maybe it was not their greater intelligence but their ability to experience that connection, to use it in some new way.

Elijah raised his hands now and rubbed them together, feeling the tingling he had come to feel whenever someone near him was sick or hurt. But he did not put his tingling hands on Landis. He could not. He would take turns with Cassie in this room, sitting by this bedside, but he would not try to keep Charles Landis from what he had brought upon himself. In whatever way the two of them were one, it did not affect the story that was unfolding between them. Landis had made one choice, and Elijah had made another.

Whenever Cassie came to tend Landis, Elijah went to Amber's room. He would wipe her forehead with an alcohol-soaked cloth and then rest his tingling hands gently on her head, his palms on her damp hair, his fingers on the burning skin of her forehead. He imagined light, brilliant white-violet light pouring through him into her body. And he felt the heat pulsing beneath his fingers. Hour after hour, he stayed with her, shifting his hands from time to time, willing her body to throw off the poison.

"If they die," Cassie told Elijah on the third day, "I won't stay. I have relatives in Canada—full-bloods—and an emergency escape plan that Charles and I worked out years ago." She looked off toward the window, but her eyes did not seem to register the gray swirl of snow outside. "You can go with me or you can stay. It's up to you."

"What about Kenny?" Elijah asked.

Cassie frowned, shaking her head. "He wouldn't leave. He's the heir to all Charles stands for." She passed a hand over her eyes. "All he stood for."

"Mack won't let you go," Elijah said. "You know too much."

"Mack won't know till I've gone. And he won't know where to look for me. No one knows the plan but Charles and me."

On the fifth day Charles Landis died. Cassie, her face a still blankness, bathed and dressed him in his uniform. "The ground is frozen too hard to bury him," she told Elijah, "but we can have his service now."

Elijah did not attend the funeral in the lodge. He stayed with Amber, his hands on her head, visualizing light.

Amber was drifting—rising from the earth into a soft, warm, shimmering darkness. As the ground dwindled away beneath her, she had no sense of danger. After a time she could make out a gleam like a moon path on water. As she focused on it, she found herself drifting toward it. Closer and closer she came until she saw that it was solid. It curved away ahead of her like a path through a star-sprinkled sky. Her feet touched it, and she began walking, one foot in front of the other.

How long she walked she couldn't tell; minutes or days, it was as if there was no time. Just one step and another, the silvery glow of the path beneath her, the dark shimmer around and above. Then she saw a figure moving ahead of her. She couldn't see the figure clearly, but she knew it was her father. She hurried toward him, trying to catch up as he moved away, but though he did not seem to change his pace, she came no closer. "Daddy!" she called, and began to run.

A swirl of fog, spangled with pinpricks of golden light, drifted across the path, enveloping him in its glittering tendrils. "Daddy!" she called again. But he was vanishing into the fog. He had neither seen nor heard her. She slowed to a walk. The fog, growing ever brighter against the dark sky, seemed to be moving toward her, reaching out for her. Some part of her longed to step into it, to follow and find her father. But something else held her back. Aware of a deep ache in the center of herself, she stopped. She watched the fog obliterate the path, and then, slowly, began to back away.

Amber opened her eyes, blinking in the bright light of her bedside lamp. Elijah's hands were hot against her forehead, his face creased with worry and concentration. Every part of her body seemed to hurt.

Elijah, dark eyes solemn, looked down at her, his hands quiet on her skin. Images filled her head. Her father in his uniform, lying on a table draped with the Militia's flag, the men ranged around him, Cassie and Kenny at his head, Mack at his feet. "He's dead, isn't he?" she asked, her voice little more than a croak through her swollen throat.

Elijah nodded.

As he did, memory returned to her in a rush. Her father's perfect plan. Biowar. Smallpox. The nightmare with its mountain of bodies. She closed her eyes again.

Each death, she thought, each single death, was a devastation to everyone who loved that person. Devastation! She had asked her father how many died in the Northway bombing, and he had had no certain answer. It didn't matter. Whatever the number of bodies, the number of people left to rearrange the shattered bits of their lives, to find a way through their grief was far, far greater. Her mother's death had changed the course of every life she had touched. If Marion Landis had not been murdered, there would have been no Militia. What would Charles Landis have done instead? What might Kenny have been like? And who, Amber wondered, would *she* have been?

Her father too was gone now, and everything would change again. The center had disappeared from Amber's world. What it would mean she didn't yet know, but she could begin to guess at the pain there would be. She felt a hole in herself so big it seemed almost larger than she was.

Her father had been wrong about the effects of the smallpox he planned to release into the world. It would *not* have taken half the human population. In some deeper way it would have taken them all.

She felt Elijah's hands lift from her forehead.

"Am I going to die too?" she asked.

"I don't think so," he said.

She nodded, the ache in her head seeming to explode at the movement. When the fog had closed around her father, something had ended. Forever. Something else, she knew, had begun.

In the weeks it took Amber to get her strength back, Mack established himself as the commander of the Free Mountain Militia. No one challenged the change. Their next operation, he had announced the day after the funeral, would be exactly the sort they had accomplished before. They would take out an underground technology center, the necessary computer hardware for a major link in the nets. "Short of knocking out a satellite," he told the men, "we could not cripple more of the system than this in a single blow." There was no mention of biowar. No mention of smallpox.

Except for the hours every morning and evening when Elijah worked at sending healing light and warmth into Amber's gradually strengthening body, he did what Cassie advised, slipping back into the wolf pack as if nothing had changed with Charles Landis's death. In fact Paradise Park seemed little different without its leader. It ran as it had before, the men looking to Mack for direction as they always had.

Only Kenny seemed to have changed, though the changes were so small Elijah thought he might be imagining them. Kenny seemed almost to have grown taller, broader, taking up more space wherever he was, the way Charles Landis had always managed to seem larger than his physical presence. There was a hint of swagger in his walk, a curve to his mouth that was like the beginning of a sneer. The faint buzz that had from the beginning alerted Elijah to Kenny's presence became a low, steady growl. Whenever possible, Elijah avoided being near him. It was not difficult, as Mack most often sent Elijah to work in the computer room while he kept Kenny busy elsewhere, helping to prepare for the assault on the underground technology center.

During those weeks Cassie went about the work she had always done, caring for the greenhouse, maintaining the netsite, planning the summer garden. But in the cottage, alone with Elijah and Amber, she explained the activation of her emergency plan.

Elijah had agreed to go along from the first mention of leaving, but neither had mentioned it to Amber until she told them about the dream she'd had while she was sick. "Something happened when I didn't go on into that fog," she told them. "I think the person who came back here isn't the person I was before." She would leave Paradise Park with them as soon as she was strong enough.

Neither Elijah nor Amber asked for details about where they were going or what they would do when they arrived. *It will be like being born,* each thought, aware that they were alike in this, *a beginning that has nothing to do with anything that went before.*

Elijah found himself watching for the raven, having to remind himself over and over that it was gone. All the ravens had disappeared. Not since the night Elijah had switched the vials had he seen one of them winging its way above the trees. That night came to seem to Elijah like Amber's dream, a turning point that separated one life from another.

One night in late April, shortly after two A.M., Cassie woke them. "This is it. The weather's perfect. Don't turn on lights," she warned. "And keep your flashlights away from the windows." Their backpacks were packed and ready. They had only to put on their double layer of clothes, their ski pants, wool socks, hiking boots, and parkas. They had planned their route out of Paradise Park carefully, and Elijah, just as when he had run away from Laurel Mountain, had disabled part of the security system.

It was snowing, a heavy, wet spring snow that came down hard and fast onto the thin layer of old snow that had melted in the last few sunny days and frozen again each night. By morning there would be no sign of their footprints. Above the cloud cover a nearly full moon lightened the world enough so that in spite of the thickly falling snow, they could move with some speed. As they hurried across the open space between the cottage and the woods, the crunching of the ice crust sounded loud in their ears.

"Are you okay?" Cassie asked Amber when they had reached the cover of the trees. "Are you going to be able to do this?"

"Of course," Amber answered firmly.

Cassie led the way with Amber behind her, Elijah in the rear. They planned to bushwhack through the woods to one of the old logging roads and follow that to the highway. A few miles along the highway there was a cabin that was closed up for the winter. There a pair of snowmobiles would be waiting for them. They expected to reach the cabin before dawn and rest awhile before starting out again.

As they walked, Elijah began to get the sensation that he was in dreamtime, not fully there in the snowy night, moving behind Amber across the crackling ice crust. He felt as if only part of himself inhabited the body that was doing these things. The rest of his awareness seemed to have moved beyond the woods of Paradise Park.

Suddenly, without having chosen to search for it, he felt the thread that connected him to Taryn. As he felt it, he felt as well her sleeping self, sensed the room around her, a room he knew was in the main lodge at Laurel

Mountain, sensed the snow swirling in the wind against her window. She was dreaming, he realized, as he slipped into her dream. She was dressed warmly, moving with speed and purpose through a tree-filled snowy night. There were dark figures moving ahead of her—not three but five, their heads bent against the wind.

With a shock of recognition Elijah saw that the nearest one was Doug. Dream connected to dream, and he knew that Doug too, asleep in a narrow, cluttered room illuminated by moonlight and filled with the city sounds of cars and distant sirens, was dreaming this trek through the Adirondack night. As Elijah moved among the figures of Doug's dream, the connection branched again to Miranda, asleep and dreaming this winter night's escape in the growing light of a distant dawn.

Elijah was swept back, then, into his body, into the snow touching his face with cold that turned wet against his skin. The Ark family was dreaming together again. What did it mean? Would the others remember the dream, the flight from Paradise Park?

Then he understood that this leaving was not flight. It was journey. And it was not a total break from all that had gone before. It was somehow part of the quest.

He'd been right all along, Kenny thought. He had warned Mack they would leave, but Mack hadn't believed him. That was because Mack didn't understand Cassie, didn't see that it had been Charles Landis and only Charles Landis who kept her with the Militia. Not the mission, not Amber, certainly not himself—only their father.

He had to admit, though, they'd been good, the three of them. They had given no sign that they were getting ready to run. Cassie had spent even this last afternoon going over the plans for expanding the vegetable garden with Ham and Duane. As if she would be there to plant it, to harvest and preserve the food for next winter. And Amber had begun going to the computer center again, updating the kidsite, returning to her on-line classes as if she expected to graduate. There had been nothing to give them away except Kenny's own instincts.

Of course it didn't matter whether Cassie and Amber left. Women were a liability in an army. But with Charles Landis gone, they might rat the Cadre out. He couldn't let that happen.

Then there was Elijah. No homemade bow and arrow this time. He shifted the weight of the deer hunting rifle he carried, its barrel pointed toward the ground. The moonlight that let the others see to get away would let him use the scope, if he could catch them in the open. It would be easy, their dark figures in the crosshairs against the gleaming snow. When this night was over, Elijah and all his genius, all his weirdness, would be gone. History.

The three of them would have to stop and rest eventually. Amber wasn't strong enough yet to go very far. If he couldn't catch them crossing open ground, he would take them out when they stopped, one after another, so fast there would be no time to react. It was the only way. The only thing to do. And he could do it. No member of the Cadre, no member of the Militia, was a better shot than Kenny.

He'd been watching the cottage for a week now, ever since Amber had been up and around, expecting Cassie to make her move as soon as she judged that the time was right. When it had begun snowing tonight, he had known that she would go if the snow kept up. He chuckled to himself, the sound no louder than the crunch under his feet. The snow they were counting on to hide their tracks had given them away. A hunter has to be smarter than his prey, he thought.

Kenny blinked snow off his eyelashes. It would be a whole new place from now on, Paradise Park. Much as he missed his father, would miss him all the rest of his life, it was Mack who really understood him, valued and trusted him. Mack knew and respected what Kenny could do as his father never had. He'd already promised that Kenny would have a place with the Cadre as long as he wanted one, until the day he was old enough to take his father's command. Mack was quite clear that day would come, and he would step aside, becoming beta wolf to Kenny's alpha.

They had gone little more than half a mile when Elijah heard the first hint of a distant growl. Kenny. He was following them. Far back yet, but following.

He stopped for a moment, straining backward to see what he could hear through the whispery quiet of wind and snow. Nothing. Amber's and Cassie's movements were too loud to let him sort out other sounds. He caught up to Amber then and tapped her on the back. "I'm going back a bit to check on something. Tell Cassie to keep going. I'll catch up."

He went back a short way along the track they had left, the new snow already softening its edges. It would be invisible by morning, he was pleased to see. He stepped behind a tree and peered into the gray-blue darkness the way they had come. After a few minutes he knew he'd been right. He could make out now the crunch of footsteps, the growing growl of Kenny's approach. He pressed himself against the tree, breathing into the rough bark, and sent his mind outward.

Kenny was moving slowly and carefully, following their trail but making no effort to catch up. As he connected, Elijah felt Kenny's excitement, his sense of triumph. Alpha wolf, Kenny believed himself to be, hunter, infinitely superior to his prey. But there was something else as well, a sharp tingle of fear as he moved between the humped, shadowy forms of snow-covered bushes, boulders, stumps, looming in the darkness. This alpha wolf had not hunted at night, when the familiar woods seemed alien and unpredictable. A low thump as snow slid from an overhead branch jolted Kenny to a stop, heart pounding as he aimed his rifle toward the sound.

Elijah pulled his awareness back to himself. There wasn't much time to decide what to do. He might jump Kenny as he came past, use the advantage of surprise to get the gun away from him. But Kenny more than outweighed him. He was taller, stronger, and trained to fight. Anger surged through Elijah. It wasn't belief that drove Charles Landis's son. It wasn't mission or meaning or even a drive for power. Kenny liked to fight, to cause pain, to kill. And this time it was clear he meant to kill.

Don't be stupid. There's nothing out there. Kenny lowered the rifle. The sound had been nothing but snow dropping from the trees. There was absolutely nothing in these woods to be afraid of, he assured himself. No predators that could not be taken easily by the gun he carried. Nothing big. The trouble was, his own assurances didn't help. It made no sense, this fear that seemed to be growing as he moved through the shifting darkness among the humps and mounds of snow.

Snow trolls. The words came to him from a past so distant he couldn't pin it down. Some baby-sitter's bedtime stories, they were, evil creatures lurking beneath the snows of the northernmost woods. *Don't be stupid,* he told himself again, holding more tightly to his rifle. Another thump, this one behind him. *Nothing but snow sliding off a pine tree!* But it was all he could do to keep himself from imagining something following him, coming closer, all he could do to keep from breaking into a run. He knew if he ran, his imagination would take over, creating a hunter about to spring on him, a nightmare image growing ever more terrifying as he ran. *I'm the hunter.* But it took every bit of discipline he could muster to keep himself moving into the thickly falling snow.

The tracks he was following split around one of the snow mounds, where two had gone to the right and one had gone left. He didn't have to worry which track to choose, he thought. His prey would not be splitting up. It was only a choice one of the three had made to take a different way around an obstacle. The tracks would join again soon enough. He took a deep breath and felt his grip on the rifle relax as he followed the right-hand trail. He was all right now. The mind of the hunter was taking control again.

Elijah stood against the tree, listening to the outward sounds of Kenny moving closer, the inward growl of his intended violence. Kenny would pass him soon. He had to decide, had to act. As the growl intensified inside his head, every painful moment of Elijah's life, every loss and fear and fury, seemed to come together like a fireball exploding upward and outward. *Bear.* The image rose in his mind, and he felt its energy pulse through his body. He felt himself expanding, shoulders and arms bulking up, fingers curving into claws. From the center of himself came a deep, rumbling roar.

Kenny stopped at the sound, a chill running up his arms and across the back of his neck. *Bear,* he thought wildly, *early out of its den.* But that made no sense. Bears did not leave their dens in the night in the snow. The sound came again, off to his left. From the deep shadow of a pine tree a figure materialized, moving through the curtain of falling snow on two thick legs, huge as a nightmare coming to life. Kenny let out a howl and tried to raise his rifle to his shoulder, but the thing was on him, knocking the gun from his grip with a single blow, flinging it into the snow well out of reach.

Kenny raised his arms as the figure swung again and felt the sharp slash of claws on his cheek, tearing the skin. He turned to run, slipped and fell, then scrambled to his feet, whimpering in terror as he lurched away. The creature followed for a time, growling and snorting, crashing through the snow and ice and underbrush. Kenny, unaware that his pursuer had stopped, fled through the darkness, feeling the blood on his cheek mingle with the melting snow.

Elijah stood very still as the sounds of Kenny's flight faded away. *I could have killed him*, he thought. *Bear or Elijah, I could have killed him*.

But you did not. The words rang in his head almost as if someone else had said them. He nodded to himself. *I did not*.

When he caught up to Amber and Cassie, who had stopped and started back toward the commotion, he did not explain. "A bear," was all he said. "There was a bear. It's gone now."

As they began to move again, a dark shape swept down out of the sky, winged its way over Elijah's head, and landed on the bare branch of a tree studded with the hard buds of leaves that would open in another month. Elijah was the only one of the three who saw it. After a moment the raven lifted itself from the branch and flew ahead of them, vanishing quickly into the falling snow.

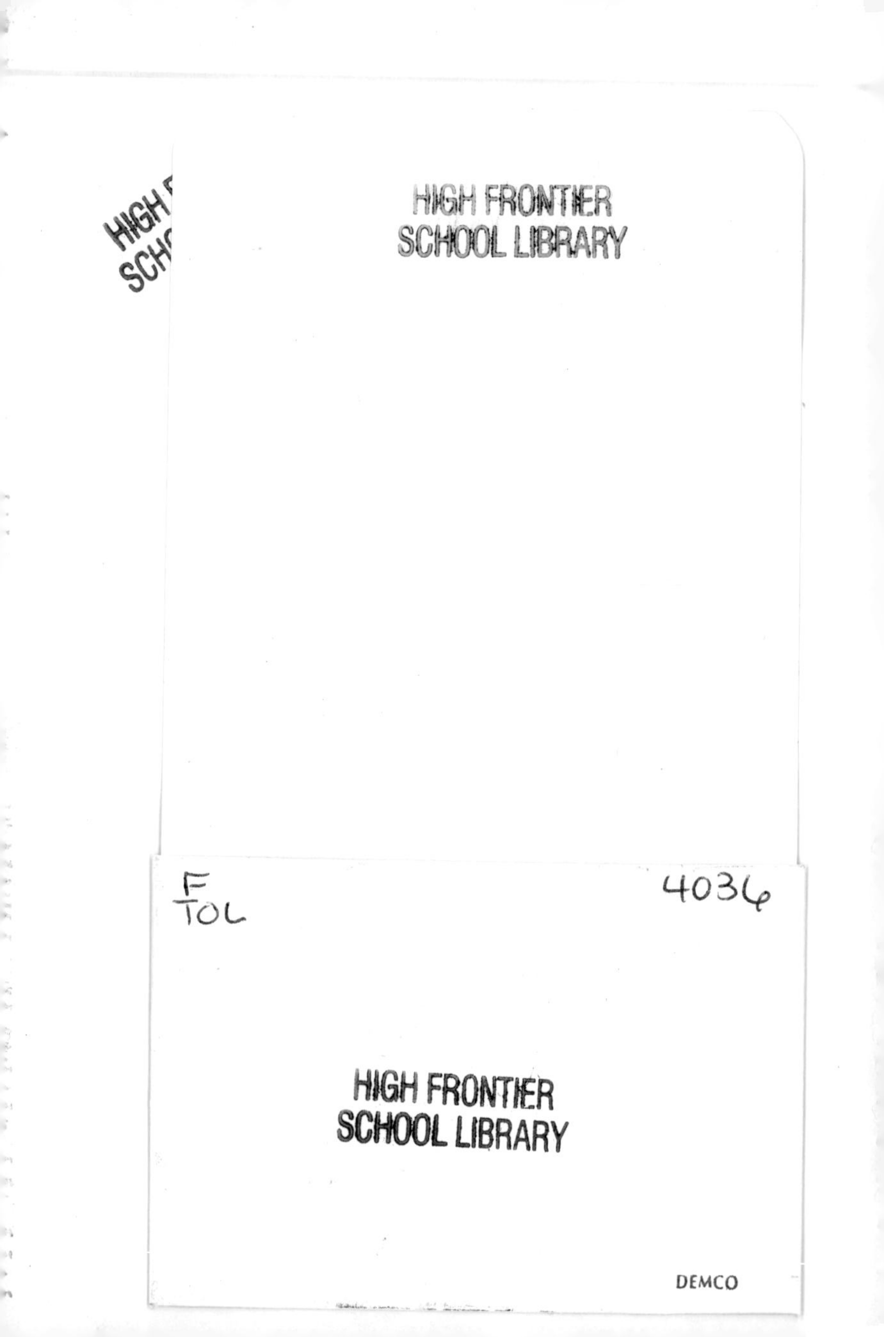

HIGH FRONTIER
SCHOOL LIBRARY

F
TOL
4036

HIGH FRONTIER
SCHOOL LIBRARY

DEMCO